The terrorist's shock was the diversion Bolan needed

He threw one leg high in the air, wrapped his thigh around the giant's neck, then sat up, straining leg muscles to pin his opponent to the ground. He continued to apply pressure, scissoring the hardman's neck between his legs.

The terrorist reached up and pulled the knife from his arm in a last-ditch effort for survival. He raised the blade to bury it in Bolan's thigh, but his movements served only to facilitate a tighter hold. The sound of vertebrae snapping in the man's neck resounded with unquestionable finality.

Bolan released the giant, panting with exhaustion. He looked at his shoulder, reminded of the injury as a fresh wave of pain washed over him. He was nauseated and close to losing consciousness. He needed food and rest, but neither of those was within his grasp. There was still an army of Kahane Chai terrorists out there somewhere that had to be stopped.

And by his calculations, the numbers were running down.

MACK BOLAN ®
The Executioner

DON PENDLETON'S
THE EXECUTIONER®
CYBERHUNT

A GOLD EAGLE BOOK FROM
WORLDWIDE®

TORONTO • NEW YORK • LONDON
AMSTERDAM • PARIS • SYDNEY • HAMBURG
STOCKHOLM • ATHENS • TOKYO • MILAN
MADRID • WARSAW • BUDAPEST • AUCKLAND

First edition June 2001
ISBN 0-373-64271-7

Special thanks and acknowledgment to
Jon Guenther for his contribution to this work.

CYBERHUNT

Man is still the most extraordinary computer of all.
                                    —President John F. Kennedy
                                    May 21, 1963

Any terrorist group that thinks it can hide behind
cybernetic technology and wreak havoc isn't safe from
me. Eventually, I'll find these cowards and unplug their
schemes with a program of my own—total destruction.
                                    —Mack Bolan

To all the victims of the Columbine High School
shooting, which took place on April 20, 1999—
may the living find peace in their grief
and the departed find eternal rest

PROLOGUE

Dr. Niles Westerbeck entered through the coded access doors of the Feynman Computing Center on a mission of importance.

The scientist was a stout, balding man with a comb-over, and he wore thick bifocals. Although quiet and unassuming as a child, Westerbeck had been labeled "too smart for his own good" by teachers and parents alike. His IQ would have put most MIT graduates to shame.

As he walked down the main corridor, Westerbeck considered the rich history of the area. The newest addition to the Fermi National Accelerator Laboratory, the Center was a three-story structure of seventy-four thousand square feet and housed the central computing facilities for the entire complex.

The grounds at Fermilab were as attractive as they were practical, with feats of modern architecture that originated with its construction beginning in the mid-1960s. Other buildings included Robert R. Wilson Hall, named after the first director. There were the scallop-shaped culverts of Meson Lab and the dome tops of Neutrino Lab. Proton Lab was a famous, pagoda-shaped building. It had a yellow spiral staircase that resembled the double-helix strand of a DNA molecule.

Westerbeck thought of the staircase as he rode the security elevator to the top floor. He was the newest director of Fermilab, and although the line of predecessors was short, it was certainly distinguished. With less than six months on the job, Westerbeck wondered if he could live up to the demands. He was in charge of one of the most advanced nuclear fission laboratories in the world, and he took the job seriously.

At the moment, Westerbeck was irritated. As he stepped from the elevator and entered the operations center, he didn't bother to hide that fact. Two men immediately rushed over to where he stood waiting.

"Gentleman, I hope you're aware I was in the middle of a lecture," Westerbeck announced. "I've got a hundred people sitting over at Ramsey Auditorium who are probably wondering what the hell is going on. So, would someone like to explain?"

The Fermilab director's eyes scanned the nearby computer screens and imaging displays. The answer to his question came before either man could conjure a reply. Westerbeck walked quickly toward one large screen, which displayed a graphic representation of the Tevatron accelerator. Multicolored lights flashed at specific points along the accelerator's pathway. Those lights winked in some very sensitive areas.

"We have a major problem, Dr. Westerbeck," Gregory Lapp said.

Lapp was Fermilab's computer operations chief, and Westerbeck trusted him implicitly. The man had worked for nearly every major electronics firm across the country, and his knowledge of computers was surpassed only by his ability to troubleshoot problems quickly.

"That sounds like an understatement," Westerbeck replied. He turned to Lapp, an expression on his face that demanded an explanation.

"We were monitoring one of the tests for those German physicists who came in last week," Lapp began. "Things were fine until we started receiving a score of error messages. We tried to commence an abort sequence, but the signal computers went haywire before we could make it happen."

Westerbeck again glanced at the imaging display. "According to these readings, we have structural collapse in five separate sections."

"Not true," Lapp said, shaking his head.

"What do you mean?"

"As soon as the computers went down, I sent a security detail and a radiation team to check it out."

"We didn't want to create a panic until we knew the true nature of the problem, Doctor," Devon Grant interjected.

Grant was the graphics-imaging expert for the Feynman Center. He had begun his career designing computer programs for a software gaming company. Westerbeck had first met him at a conference in Dallas. He was so impressed with the young man's knowledge and likable personality that he hired him on the spot. Westerbeck was a good judge of character, and he never regretted his decision to bring Grant to Fermilab.

"There are no breaches or structural collapses of any kind," Lapp continued.

Westerbeck jabbed his finger at the display. "That's *not* what this says, Greg."

"We know that, sir. Look, half of the network says everything checks out and the other half shows readings off the board. It's like the whole system's developed a mind of its own."

"Well, we all know better than that," Westerbeck shot back. "Computers do what they're told to do. They don't have personality flaws, so it has to be some kind of glitch."

"The false readings aren't the worst part," Grant said. "We're more concerned with the fact we can't stop the test we were monitoring."

Westerbeck felt a headache coming on as he considered the gravity of Grant's statement. In all his years as a nuclear physicist, he'd never truly considered the far-reaching consequences of a fission accident. Visions of Fermilab erupting into a mushroom cloud danced in front of his eyes.

The general public didn't consider playing with atomic particles sane behavior to begin with.

The Tevatron accelerator was only one component of a much larger and complex system. Atomic and subatomic matter traveled along a circular path at speeds greater than light. They collided inside the accelerator, and like any object of kinetic energy, they continued in motion until acted upon by an outside force. The dampers were such a force, but they were the only fail-safes capable of dissipating the tremendous energies created by nuclear fission. Any other attempt to defuse the test could likely result in an explosive force of twelve 500-megaton bombs.

Grant turned to look at the back of a technician seated at a partially darkened console.

"Do we have any communications at all, Ken?" he asked the technician.

"No, sir," Ken replied. He didn't let his eyes leave the console. As he stabbed buttons and switches, he added, "Only thing that might work now is the backup system."

Westerbeck stared hard at Lapp as he considered their predicament. "Can we backtrack this thing to its source, Greg? Maybe we can run a diagnostic."

"I doubt it." Lapp's features were taut with a thin-lipped frown. "Automatic fail-safe won't respond, manual overrides are off-line and—"

Bright flashes of light erupted on the imaging display, followed by darkness. Every light in the operations room winked out. Grant leaned down to an intercom to call for emergency power. The trio stood frozen and silent. Almost a minute passed before the center was bathed in the blue-and-yellow hues of overhead emergency lights.

It seemed as if everyone in the center released a simultaneous sigh of relief.

"What the hell is going on?" Lapp wondered aloud.

"Could this be a virus of some kind?" Grant asked.

"If it is," Westerbeck replied, "it's going to take some time to figure out the how and why of the damned thing."

He turned to Lapp. "Start implementing grounds-wide emergency protocols. Tell security to clear every laboratory, every building, the works. Notify residents at Fermilab Village to evacuate, as well."

Lapp nodded and proceeded to initiate the alert.

Westerbeck wheeled to face Grant. "Get over to the power station. See if you can find out how long it's going to be before they can restore power. Stay in contact with me at all times."

Grant turned, walked quickly to a nearby cabinet and pulled a flashlight and portable radio from it. He entered his access code, and the door leading out of the center slid aside obediently. Grant tossed a look of relief at Westerbeck before he left.

Westerbeck jumped as alarms began to sound throughout the complex. He hoped everyone responded as they had been trained. Fermilab conducted regular drills, but the director couldn't seem to find a tremendous amount of solace in that thought. He didn't wish to compound the problem, but he had the lives of hundreds of personnel to consider.

While it was still too early to notify outside authorities, Westerbeck considered the idea. If they couldn't find the source of this shutdown quickly, he would have to contact the local fire and police departments, as well as the Illinois State Police HazMat Unit.

Provided the Tevatron's structural integrity held—and he had no reason to believe otherwise—there was no immediate danger. He had every confidence in Lapp and Grant. They would figure it out. In the meantime, he would have to remain calm and work on the problem.

His eye caught a red telephone mounted to a nearby wall. It was a direct line to the Pentagon.

God help us all, Westerbeck thought.

1

What Mack Bolan craved was a little R&R—maybe a week of skiing, or hiking through the mountains. Something to restore mind and body. A recent mission with his brother Johnny had taxed his resources to the limit. Fences had been mended, and now it was time to renew the spirit.

However, what the Executioner got was another mission.

Over the years, Hal Brognola had asked Bolan to meet him in many locations for a sitdown, but this was the first time in a long while that an airport was the venue. And this time Barbara Price was with the big Fed. An international conference on satellite communication systems had brought them to the state.

Bolan, a.k.a. the Executioner, glanced through the large, rain-specked window of the terminal. Months had passed since his last visit to Colorado, but little had changed. A flurry of ground-crew activity moved in and out of view against a backdrop of gray fog. Lights from landing planes pierced the gloom. It was unusual weather for June in the Rockies, particularly considering the dry mountain climate. Nonetheless, the Mile High City bustled on, despite a little inclement weather.

Bolan checked his watch, and decided to let another minute pass. Finally, he rose from his chair in the seating area and strolled toward a gray metal door that was set in a wall on the opposite side of the terminal walkway. As he approached the door, Bolan remembered the prearranged signal. The door was usually locked. Stony Man's connections reached far and wide, and arrangement had been made with an airport security guard on the payroll. If the door was open, the meeting was on. If not, he would walk away and forget the whole thing.

Bolan felt naked without the trusted Beretta 93-R in shoulder leather under his arm. He certainly had enough phony credentials to get him past the checkpoints, but he'd elected to forego this option. Employing such a tactic would have only served to alert possible observers, and Bolan preferred to use the element of surprise.

He pushed through the door and entered a long hallway. It was a service corridor of some kind, which terminated at a T-intersection. A door across the hall granted him outside access.

The Executioner followed the directions from memory, turning up the collar of his leather jacket to protect himself from the cool mist. He jogged a course unnoticed through the fog and maintained the pace until a small hangar came into view. It was set two hundred yards beyond the farthermost runway. The building was constructed of corrugated steel and painted as gray as the fog that shrouded it. There were no windows, but Bolan found a door on the opposite side of the building and opened it just enough to slide inside.

The hangar was deserted.

Years of disuse were obvious from the thick layer of dust that covered the macadam floor. The interior was deathly quiet and poorly lit. Two pairs of footprints were visible in the dust. Bolan followed them to a narrow office. He pressed his ear against the thin metal of the door and heard the echo of voices.

He quietly entered the room, and a pair of familiar faces turned toward him. Hal Brognola and Barbara Price looked startled initially, but their expressions visibly relaxed when they recognized the specterlike form of the Executioner.

"Good to see you, Striker," Brognola boomed.

The soldier moved over to the long metal table where they were seated, returning Brognola's greeting with a nod. The big Fed pointed toward one of the remaining four seats arranged unevenly along the table. Bolan pulled one over and dropped into it. He smiled at Price, who returned it with a knowing grin.

Brognola got right to business. "I appreciate you meeting us like this, Striker."

"It sounded important when we talked last," Bolan replied easily.

"It is. The President has given this top priority, and I was instructed to use any means at my disposal. He knows you're involved."

The remark wasn't lost on Bolan. "What's up?"

"I'll let Barbara get us started, since she's up-to-date on what precipitated this whole thing."

Price acknowledged Brognola, then focused her complete attention on Bolan. She was beautiful beyond words, but she was also a pure professional. The job of mission controller for Stony Man was an important one, and Bolan could think of nobody more competent than the woman now seated in front of him.

"Forty-eight hours ago, the Pentagon sent a top secret report that something went berserk with the main computer systems at the Fermi National Accelerator Laboratory in Batavia, Illinois. Are you familiar with the facility?"

"Vaguely," Bolan replied. "If memory serves, they conduct nuclear fission experiments using particle-accelerator technology."

"And that's just the tip of the iceberg," Brognola supplied.

"At the behest of the Oval Office," Price continued, "we sent Aaron to assist them with the problem."

"Well, if anyone can get to the heart of the matter, the Bear can," Bolan said. "Do we know exactly what happened?"

Price shook her head. "Too early to say, but this whole matter sparked a larger interest. Fermilab was conducting experiments of a more sensitive nature. There were only two people privy to this information—the director of the site, Dr. Niles Westerbeck, and their computer chief, Gregory Lapp.''

"Something you may not know," Brognola interjected, "is that the shutdown occurred inside the Feynman Computing Center. A majority of the funds used to construct this building were allocated by the federal government. In exchange, Westerbeck agreed to test a new 64-bit encryption computer chip under very secretive conditions.''

"Let me guess," Bolan growled. "They think the chips caused this problem.''

"Not at all," Price stated. "We're sure the two incidents are completely unrelated. The problem isn't the technology itself, but the reason behind its use.''

"I don't follow.''

Price retrieved a thick folder from the briefcase next to her chair and opened it. She thumbed through the first couple of pages until she found the information she was obviously searching for, and began to read from a page of notes.

"About eighteen months ago, the Senate Arms Committee approved the export of 64-bit chip technology to allied governments and what they called, quote, 'responsible research facilities.' Until recently, the reasons behind this were a closely guarded secret, even from Stony Man. It apparently stemmed from a paper published by the International Policy Institute for Counterterrorism.''

"They're a relatively new group, right?" Bolan asked.

"Yes. They were established in 1996 as an international think tank, so their work is largely abstract.''

"Nevertheless, they have some great minds working for them," Brognola added, "and when they talk, Congress listens. Their aim has always been to develop counterterrorism methods, which governments worldwide can then implement into practical applications.''

"This particular paper raised some eyebrows, Mack," Price said, "because it delved into the use of computers to wreak internal havoc. They have even coined the term *cyberterrorism* to illustrate the widespread threat. With the right technology, terrorist groups across the globe could throw entire countries into turmoil. Imagine the effect in today's society if terrorists were able to shift entire economic holdings or political agendas with little more than the push of a button.''

Bolan nodded grimly. ''Not to mention that many of America's computers provide basic needs and monitor large power systems.''

''That's the most frightening thought,'' Brognola agreed. ''We think Fermilab was just a small example of what a terrorist group could accomplish. What do you think would happen if someone decided to wipe out an organization as large as, say, the Tennessee Valley Authority?'' He raised his eyebrows and waved his hand for emphasis. ''Public utilities aside, let's consider places like NORAD or even military and nuclear installations. Even with the security measures in our own backyard, these people could drop a bombshell big enough to wipe out systems back at the Farm.''

''This is a tough piece,'' the Executioner stated. ''My methods are effective when the enemy is right in front of my eyes, because I can cut out the heart of the organization. But to eliminate terrorists hiding behind a blinking cursor is another game entirely.''

''Which brings us to the mission,'' Price replied.

She pulled a black-and-white photograph from the folder and handed it to Bolan. He studied the photo with interest. Although it was a grainy, computer-generated composite, the features of the subject left no doubt he was Middle Eastern. The man in the photo had a rounded forehead with a strong chin. The expression was pleasant, and there was the unmistakable glint of intelligence behind his dark, widely set eyes.

''That's Baram Herzhaft,'' Price announced. ''He's a computer programmer and research analyst with Mossad's counterintelligence section. As you know, the Israeli government has been taking quite a bit of heat over the past few years. Mossad has bungled one assassination attempt after another on some pretty big names in the world of terrorism. To date, their efforts have been less than effective.''

"With the problems over there, you can't really fault them,'' Bolan said.

"True, but the lack of efficiency in their methods seems to be exponential,'' Brognola countered.

"Dr. Herzhaft is frustrated by his government's failures, as are many others within their intelligence community,'' Price explained. "As a result, he has developed a machine that uses 64-bit encryption chips. He has offered to share this technology with the U.S.''

Bolan was immediately suspicious. "Why?''

"Primarily because the Arms Committee has eased those export restrictions.''

"And also because of the tremendous profits?'' Bolan offered.

Price shrugged. "That could be a factor, as well. Dr. Herzhaft calls this the Anti-Cyberterrorism Network device. ACTEN, for short. There's nothing special about 64-bit computer chips. Most computer gaming companies use them regularly in their software.''

"According to Aaron,'' Brognola said, "any first-year computer programmer or software hacker can crack the code on an encrypted 32-bit chip, and these aren't much more difficult. The 128-bit chips are said to be impossible, but Herzhaft says he can do the same with only 64 bits.''

"A foolproof system?'' Bolan asked, raising his eyebrows and returning his gaze to the picture.

"We were skeptical, as well,'' Price said. "Nevertheless, the President is prepared to give it a try. Aaron believes it's possible, and if the ACTEN device is everything Herzhaft claims it is, the cyberterrorists are going to be out of business.''

"It sounds like you may have solved the problem already,'' Bolan replied. "Where do I fit in?''

"The chips are currently secured at Fort Carson, right here

in Colorado. In two days, they'll be flown out under tight security. The final destination is Israel, although the exact location of the rendezvous is unknown.''

Price reached into the file folder and handed Bolan a second still of high quality, as well as a thin packet of information.

"This is Lieutenant Colonel Ephram Jacoby. Career soldier and highly decorated Green Beret, with countless missions into hostile territory. He's seen action in Laos, Cambodia, Central and South America, Lebanon and the Middle East. He speaks Hebrew fluently, and he was brought up in a Jewish family. He was the perfect choice to lead the escort team, and he'll be your liaison.''

"Liaison to what?''

"You'll be posing as an adviser to the SAC Chairman. You'll use the Colonel Rance Pollack cover, and you're strictly Wonderland material, so put on your best bureaucratic face.''

"I'll try,'' Bolan promised.

"There's something else you need to know, Striker,'' Brognola said. "Have you ever heard of the Kahane Chai?''

"They were officially declared a terrorist organization by the Israeli cabinet in 1994,'' Bolan recited from memory. "Basically, they're Jewish fundamentalists with a very mean streak. They're obsessed with the eradication of the Palestinians from Hebron and the restoration of Israel as a biblical state.''

"That's it in a nutshell.'' Brognola didn't appear surprised at Bolan's knowledge. "The Kahane Chai is actually a spin-off of Kach, which was founded by the Israeli-American rabbi Meir Kahane. Their activities are of particular interest to the Anti-Defamation League, which has never denied claims they are a propaganda arm of the Israeli government. Mossad expected there might be some trouble from the Kahane Chai, though. While there's no evidence of Kahane activity here, it's no secret they have a load of supporters in both the U.S. and Europe. There's also the threat from the Palestinians, particularly Hamas, but the Israelis are convinced the Kahane might try to make a grab for this technology.''

''That doesn't sound plausible, Hal,'' Bolan replied. ''The ACTEN device sounds like it would improve Israeli security against Islamic terrorists. It doesn't make much sense to consider the Kahane a threat.''

''Maybe not,'' Brognola said with a shrug, ''but that's where their main concerns lie. In any case, Mossad has placed an agent inside the escort group. This individual is posing as a linguistics expert, but we don't know who he is or how to contact him.''

''Mossad wasn't that amenable to cooperating with us,'' Price added, ''and they refused to give us any more information.''

''Are they concerned we might blow the agent's cover?'' Bolan asked.

''Possibly, but we can't be sure. Given the importance of this technology, they're going to protect their investment and consider any outsiders as a potential threat.''

''Politics,'' Bolan muttered.

''You'll have to keep your eyes open and wait for the right time to make contact, Striker,'' Brognola said.

''I'm not sure I like that idea. I prefer to work alone. But if Mossad's not willing to cooperate, I guess I'll have to play it by ear.''

Brognola offered him a sympathetic expression. ''The bottom line is that our goals are united. It's really quite simple. Make sure the transfer of the chips goes off without a hitch. I don't have to say that secrecy is of the utmost importance here.''

Bolan was feeling the air of tension that had settled on the meeting. Cyberterrorism. The very name sent a chill up his spine. The thought of fighting a nameless, faceless enemy— especially without the benefit of tangible leads or hard intelligence—was enough to set the Executioner's teeth on edge.

It posed a whole new challenge to his straightforward approach of identify, isolate, destroy.

The soldier knew he was walking into a potentially lethal situation. It wouldn't be the first time. He would be on his own soil, and in a military element, but there the similarities ended. Everything else was unknown. The intelligence was weak and the mission was replete with ambiguities, but there was nothing he could do about that. He would have to play by the rules.

And if all else failed, the Executioner would make up some rules of his own.

2

The Border between Jordan and Israel

Jurre Mendel watched the soldiers with anticipation of the coming mission.

The most important consideration was getting the American technology off the U.S. Army base. Once the chips were loaded onto the stolen C-141 parked on the airstrip below, it wouldn't be terribly difficult to fly the plane out of America. That was where the success of the Kahane Chai hinged upon his leadership.

The setting sun baked the salt and sand flats of their camp. Mendel stood upon the parapet of the observation tower, the only visible point above the Kahane Chai's bunker headquarters. The camp was located in the desert region bordering Israel and Jordan. They had built a small underground complex beneath the desert, shielded from satellite and infrared photography. The tower was made from sandstone, designed like the great wailing towers of Mendel's Jewish ancestors. The airstrip was actually a series of thin, nonreflective panels, presently coated with a two-inch layer of sand.

It was an unusual area of operation for the Kahane Chai, but the task at hand called for such measures. The Kach-Kahane movement operated primarily on the West Bank settlements and focused its aims toward the Qiryat Arba in Hebron. Agents also worked in Jerusalem and Tel Aviv, trying to convert to their cause any Israeli government official who might listen to them.

For years, the Kach and Kahane Chai had tried peaceable methods to restore Israel. The Jews were God's chosen people, and that was for good reason. The Kahane Chai was restless now, and Binyamin Kahane was calling for methods that were more permanent. Even the Israel Defense Forces were troubled. The Kach-Kahane movement had increased its acts against the Palestinians, and carried out threats of assassination against several high-ranking officials within the Israeli government itself.

Mendel didn't necessarily agree with killing his own kind, but he was a soldier and he obeyed orders.

The general population didn't understand the need for decisive action. Threatening to bomb the Temple Mount or Al-Aqsa Mosque was admirable, but it did nothing to truly further the Kach-Kahane aims. Eradication of the Palestinians was an end to justify the means. Too much innocent blood had been shed—Jewish blood. Mendel wouldn't allow the grounds of his own country to be fertile with the wasted remains of his people.

It wasn't as if the Israeli government had heard their cries. Rabbi Ra'nan had been murdered in cold blood in Tel Rumeida. The entire incident was a spectacle, and the arrival of the supposedly concerned members of the Israeli cabinet nothing more than a public-relations fiasco. Members of the Kach and Kahane Chai were unimpressed with Israel's response to such atrocities.

Shortly, that would all change.

Mendel watched as the C-141 was towed into position. In a few hours, he would be on that plane and bound for the United States. He could barely hold back his excitement. With the new computer technology in their hands, they would strike a blow against the Palestinians. It would surpass any feeble attempts by the Israeli government to repel the conspirators. They would purge the country of every Arab, and there would no longer be any reason to fear reprisal. The enemy would be thrown into such internal chaos that the backlash would be felt for the next century.

Mendel closed his eyes and enjoyed the hot wind as it blew against the sweat on his face. According to the Kahane Chai plan, the Palestinians would experience a complete shutdown of their systems. There would be no economic holdings, no political position. Their entire financial stability would collapse. They would be stripped of necessities such as water, oil, fuel and food. Moreover, they would lose their ability to barter for weapons and explosives.

In essence, they would cease to exist.

Worldwide response would be tumultuous. Without tangible goods, whole governments providing support would abandon the Palestinians, leave them to waste away in the sand like the carcasses of animals. They would be pickings for the Kach-Kahane movement, as if nothing more than spoiled meat for a desert carrion.

It would be a crushing blow—the final blow. The Kahane Chai would do what its people hadn't been able to do for hundreds of years. It would destroy the very fabric of Arabic society, then seize the spoils of war. The countenance of Jehovah would return to Mendel's people, and Israel would again be great!

Mendel whirled and descended the stairs within the tower. As he moved beneath ground level and entered the bunker, the temperature dropped considerably. A chill washed over him as the sweat on his muscular body began to cool against his skin. The new desert-khaki fatigue pants and short-sleeved shirt he wore enhanced his athletic physique. The pants were tucked into Israeli commando boots, and a red scarf was tied loosely around his neck and tucked into his shirtfront.

Mendel proceeded along a narrow corridor, stopping before a wooden door. He unslung his Galil rifle and handed it to the guard standing nearby, and then his Jericho 941 pistol, admonishing the guard to take care of the weapons. They were the only remaining items that reminded Mendel of his lineage—a legacy from his father.

Gamaliel Mendel had served with the Israel Defense Forces for thirty-two honorable years. He'd been a regimental commander during the Six Day War, and led numerous covert operations as a decorated soldier. He was feared and respected by his men, recognized as a cunning warrior with a fierce spirit. He had died in the Oman Desert from infection before he could be sent to a field hospital. His blood had been spilled during some secret mission, riddled by bullets from the weapons of a nameless enemy.

Jurre Mendel had inherited his father's weapons when a comrade who had fought beside Gamaliel sought out the youth and passed the weapons on to him—the result of a sworn oath to a dying man.

Mendel knocked on the door and immediately entered when he heard a muffled reply. The room beyond was small and cramped, simply furnished with a field desk made of metal and canvas. A large map of the area where Mendel would be operating in America was pinned to the wall. Behind the field desk sat a wisp of a man, who looked up and grinned when Mendel entered.

Ben-aryeh Pessach was the Kahane Chai commander, a soldier and leader who reminded Mendel very much of his father. Pessach had a commanding presence and carried himself with an authority that demanded notice. He was the right-hand man of the organization's leader. If it came from Pessach, it was coming from the top and Mendel was proud to serve under him.

"Jurre," Pessach said warmly. He rose from his chair and hugged the man in the ceremonial fashion of the Kahane Chai brotherhood.

The men sat down, Jurre taking a chair in one corner as Pessach returned to his seat.

"Everything is proceeding as planned," Jurre announced. "I will be leaving for America on schedule."

"Good, good," Pessach replied. His expression became serious. "Has there been any more word from Baram Herzhaft?"

"I am scheduled to meet with him in four hours." Mendel paused a moment before continuing. "Are you certain about this plan, Ben-aryeh? I am uncomfortable with the thought of liquidating such a vital asset to our cause."

Pessach shook his head. "It cannot be helped, Jurre. Binyamin has insisted on complete secrecy." He waved his hand. "Besides, you will be on the plane by the time we undertake the assassination. There is nothing to worry about."

"I am not worried," Jurre said quietly. "I am simply trying to look ahead. How do we know the American technology will work?"

"Do you view Herzhaft favorably?" Pessach asked slyly.

"I view him as insurance should anything go wrong with this ACTEN device."

"I see."

"Please, Ben-aryeh, I mean no disrespect. You know how much I respect you. Nevertheless, I do not consider it wise to kill Herzhaft until we know for certain our plans against the Palestinians will succeed."

"We have our orders," Pessach replied simply. "Please keep me informed of any new developments. I should wish to hear from you again when you have returned from your meeting with Herzhaft."

"As you wish, Ben-aryeh."

Jerusalem

THE FERMILAB TEST had been a complete success!

Dr. Baram Herzhaft could hardly contain his excitement. If it worked that well on the Americans, it would be twice as effective against the Palestinians. They would never know what hit them. His government would never have to fear reprisal, because the ACTEN device was a two-way network. It would counter any cyberterrorist attacks in the same way it initiated them.

Yes, ACTEN was a truly formidable weapon.

Herzhaft rose from his seat and quickly filed his notes in the safe. The furnishings in his office at Mossad headquarters were meager but adequate. A computer terminal was built into his desk, with the actual CPU hidden from view underneath. Only Herzhaft had access to the ACTEN computer. Anyone trying to access the data-storage system would trigger a virus program, which would fry the internal circuits.

Herzhaft supported his government, but he didn't trust its members. Mossad's repeated failures in counterterrorism were embarrassing. How many innocent people had been slaughtered? How many Jews would have to die before Israel did something? The members of the Israeli cabinet sat on their heels while groups like the PLO and Hamas wreaked destruction and terror. Political tensions in the Middle East were at an all-time high, and still his government did nothing.

If everything went according to plan, the Kahane Chai would do something. Allying himself with radical fundamentalists like Jurre Mendel wouldn't have been Herzhaft's first choice. The ACTEN device would only stop cyberterrorism from a defensive standpoint. Swift action called for an offensive, and Herzhaft didn't have those kinds of connections. He would turn over the ACTEN device technology to those groups worthy of its power. The best defense was a good offense, and ACTEN was a tool for the plan that the Kahane leaders had in mind.

Herzhaft locked his office and left the Mossad building nestled in the central area of Jerusalem. His meeting with Mendel was still a couple of hours away, but he wanted to allow plenty of time to eat. Besides, he had another meeting of importance. There was new information on their agent planted in Colorado.

Herzhaft arrived at the small café a few blocks from headquarters. The room was crowded and smoky with the haze of Turkish cigarettes. The filthy eatery wouldn't have been Herzhaft's kind of place under normal circumstance, but he understood the need for his contact to maintain anonymity. Herzhaft shouldn't have been privy to information on the field operation. It was supposed to be a Mossad secret. The very thought was a joke. Mossad had trouble keeping secrets, which was probably one of the biggest reasons for its past failures.

Herzhaft quickly found his contact, and the two left the café proper for a quiet back room. The place was small but served its purpose. Herzhaft knew the man only as Esdras. He was short, thin and dressed in a pair of tan shorts with a white cotton shirt. The traditional headdress of a small religious order covered his head. His dark eyes studied Herzhaft with resolute paranoia.

"I do not have long," Esdras said.

"We are both on tight schedules, then," Herzhaft replied. "What do you know?"

"I am happy to report that Ilia is okay. Her cover is still secure among the American soldiers, and no one suspects her. She did report that she has not yet located the moles placed by Hamas."

"How did you manage to come by this information?" Herzhaft asked.

Esdras smiled coolly and shrugged. "You know better than that, Baram. I cannot reveal my sources. I can only tell you what they report."

"How do I know your information is accurate?"

"You would not have come to me if you were in doubt," Esdras pointed out.

Herzhaft swore softly with the knowledge that what Esdras had said was true. He wasn't concerned with the accuracy of the news. He was solely concerned with the safety of Ilia. She was like a daughter to him. He had trained her, nurtured her skills within the Mossad. He had many hopes for her success—as many hopes as he had worries for her welfare. She was on a very dangerous mission with no true support.

"What is wrong?" Esdras asked. "You look ill."

"It is nothing," Herzhaft mumbled. "I was not aware my people would keep me in the dark about Ilia when I recommended her for this assignment."

"I do not pretend to understand Mossad, or the reasons behind some of their decisions. I do understand your frustration."

"Do you, Esdras?"

"Yes, of course."

"I am shrouded in secrecy, sworn to protect the security of Israel *and* protect its interests. Yet with all they have entrusted to my care, they do not themselves trust me."

"You are giving them even less reason now," Esdras countered. He looked around and lowered his voice, although it was obvious they were alone. "You have engaged the help of the Kahane Chai. They have butchered hundreds by their own admission and yet you support them." He sat back and folded his arms. "Why should Mossad trust you?"

Herzhaft's eyes narrowed. "Who told you this?"

"It does not matter. It matters only that I know." Esdras stood and jabbed a finger at Herzhaft. "You now have the information requested. We are even, and this is the final meeting between us. I will not see you again."

Esdras rose and left him to sit alone.

Herzhaft was disturbed by their meeting. If Esdras knew about his affiliation with Mendel, he couldn't help but wonder if someone inside Mossad knew, as well. Selling governmental secrets was considered an act of treason. If Herzhaft was discovered, he would surely be executed. Mossad's involvement would probably not even dictate a trial. Herzhaft would just disappear.

The ACTEN device was his only insurance.

Yes, he would have to submit some kind of report to his superiors. He would tell them he hit a snag and it would take him a few days to work it out. He had that long. The rendezvous for the chips was still almost five days away. It would give him enough to time to get his affairs in order. Then he would flee Israel. Herzhaft had wondered if it would come to this, but now he was certain. When the transaction was ready to take place, Herzhaft would make the necessary arrangements. Then he would escape from Israel, never to return.

The thought pierced his heart like a knife.

IT WAS DARK by the time Herzhaft arrived in the southern quarter of Jerusalem. He checked his watch as he entered the small park of olive trees that overlooked the main highway into the city. The lights of the few cars that moved steadily along that major stretch of road were barely visible in the distance. He looked around as he walked. The silence was almost deafening. Mendel was always punctual, and Herzhaft could feel the first twinge of panic in his gut.

The sudden movement of a shadow from behind one of the trees startled Herzhaft. He relaxed when he recognized the dark outline of Jurre Mendel, silhouetted by a distant street lamp. Herzhaft continued to walk slowly as Mendel fell into step next to him. The men descended a grassy knoll and stopped at the edge of a pond bed.

Mendel looked around briefly before speaking. "Who did you meet with earlier today?"

Herzhaft couldn't disguise his expression of shock.

"I asked you a question," Mendel pressed.

"What does it matter?" Herzhaft challenged. He stood there defiantly, but it was obvious Mendel wasn't fooled by the charade.

"Do not play games with me, Herzhaft," Mendel said coldly. "I may be the only thing standing between you and a journey into eternity."

"I do not wish to argue with you," Herzhaft replied. "The man I saw is a friend, and the content of our discussion has nothing to do with this matter."

"I would disagree," Mendel said, "if I thought there was a point. You see, we already know who he is."

"Why ask me, then?"

"Because we want assurances that you are still on our side."

"You have my word," Herzhaft said, "and that will have to be enough for now."

"Your word will never be enough," Mendel snarled. "This man is a rogue agent with the Mossad and a known enemy of the Kahane Chai. If you had not been in a public place, I would have slit his throat myself."

"This poses a more interesting question, Jurre," Herzhaft said. "Why are you following me?"

"The Kahane Chai have many friends. I have many friends, as well." A subtle hint of anger flashed in Mendel's eyes as he continued, "I also have many enemies. It is my business to know who I can trust, and also to know where all of the people I know fit into the brotherhood of the Kahane Chai. Especially when it affects our cause."

"I tested the ACTEN device," Herzhaft stated. "It will do just as I claim it will, but I need certain, well, assurances before I can turn it over to the Kahane."

"What kind of assurances?"

"I want it perfectly clear that nothing is to happen to Ilia Yasso."

Mendel spit on the ground. "A Mossad witch who does not have the vision of my leader. Her loyalties lie with the government, not with us."

"But she has my loyalties, and you can do nothing without me." Herzhaft looked into the darkness, and added, "I want your personal guarantee that she will return with you in good condition."

Mendel appeared to seriously consider the request.

Herzhaft had no way to insure Mendel would keep his promise, but it made him feel better to hear it. Herzhaft would do everything in his power to make sure Ilia came back to Israel intact. Once that was accomplished, he would send for her and the two of them would live happily together in another country. He would protect Ilia. She would never have to worry about her children growing up amid the violence and continuous threat of terrorism. He loved her like a daughter, but he couldn't stifle his romantic feelings, as well. Indeed there was an age difference, but Herzhaft could live with this, and Ilia would reciprocate when she learned of his true feelings.

"I cannot make such guarantees," Mendel finally replied. "The ultimate goal is the mission, and even I am expendable. If there is some way for me to extract her, I will do it."

"Then I accept that as sufficient," Herzhaft said.

The Mossad scientist reached into his coat and handed Mendel a small computer disk. It contained the instructions and details for the rendezvous, and reiterated his terms regarding Ilia. The plan was short and simple. Herzhaft would send a representative of his choosing to the rendezvous site outside the city. The chips would then be loaded into a truck and taken by the Kahane Chai, and an alternate group of fabricated chips would be sent to Mossad headquarters as planned.

"You will not be present for the exchange?" Mendel asked with surprise.

"No," Herzhaft said, shaking his head. "It would not be good for me to be absent from my laboratory. Too many people would be suspicious. Everything you need to know is contained within that disk. Beyond that, I must maintain an appearance at the Mossad."

"I understand," Mendel replied.

He wondered if Mendel did.

3

Colorado

Yusef Nahum was ready. In less than six hours, phase two of the operation would be under way. The escort at Fort Carson would never know what hit them. Nahum's men had exceeded his expectations. There was still a considerable amount of work to be done on the airstrip in preparation for Jurre Mendel's arrival, but they would meet the deadline.

These thoughts were foremost in Nahum's mind as he studied a map of the area. He was seated inside a canvas tent that served as a command post on the edge of the operations area. The airstrip clearing was nestled near the San Isabel Forest, southwest of Cañon City. The furrows and canyons of the Sangre de Cristo Mountains loomed in the distance, and the call of nocturnal animals echoed in the approaching night.

Nahum could hear the incessant babble of Grey Creek, which ran directly through the operations area. The pilots of the stolen C-141 that would bring Mendel were reported to be the best in the Kahane Chai. Nahum hoped this was true. They would have just enough runway to put down and take off with almost no margin for error. The slightest miscalculation would dump the cargo plane into the creek.

According to the plan, the chips would be transported to Royal Gorge Park, a tourist site a few kilometers north of the operations area. The crew would then move the crates down the Arkansas River to where it met Grey Creek, and off-load them for the trip to Israel. Nahum was confident the plan would work. The Americans had foolishly done the Kahane Chai a favor by running the operation through Fort Carson.

Only one issue disturbed him. Jurre Mendel had sent a communiqué regarding the Mossad agent planted at Carson. The woman was to be kept alive at all costs. Nahum would obey his orders, but if Ilia Yasso met with any unfortunate accidents, such were the misfortunes of war. Dealing with the pompous American colonel in charge of the operation would be bad enough without having to worry about the Israeli woman.

Nahum hated the Mossad. They were pawns and puppets of the government. When they failed, the Jewish people failed. The Israeli politicians always blamed those failures on the Mossad. It seemed that everyone had a plan for counteracting the Palestinian threat, but nobody wanted to take responsibility when the plan went awry. Such vanity incensed Nahum. His superiors in the Kahane expected their subordinates to accept the consequences of failure. It left no indecision and established a pattern of both equality and stability in the ranks. Nahum had never failed Mendel or Ben-aryeh Pessach. To do so would probably push him into committing suicide. He believed in the cause of the Jewish nation *and* the sovereignty of its people. Soon, the terrorists of the Arab world would pay for their atrocities and crimes.

Soon.

Nahum sat back in his chair and looked at his watch. It was time to go. He neatly folded the map book and operations plans and tucked them in an ammo can. The air was crisp and fresh as he stepped outside the command center. His chest nearly burst out of the camouflage fatigues he wore. The fatigues were marked with U.S. identification and the rank of a colonel. It was just part of the ruse.

Nahum had allowed himself plenty of time to make the rendezvous, which would take place at the mock village. If all went as planned, the post commander would have the entire installation sealed up tight. Nahum's group would make its way up Highway 115 to the rear gate. The highway was a narrow two-lane road that bordered the rear of Fort Carson. When the "emergency" occurred, the predictable Lieutenant Colonel Jacoby would likely move the chips off the post via that route. Nahum would already be there to take command of the convoy.

Everything was proceeding on schedule. Nahum's men would have the airstrip finished—there was nothing more he could do there. His paramount duty was to seize the American technology as soon as possible. Jurre had insisted Nahum be there to supervise that phase of the operation. If the hand of Jehovah was with them, they would succeed in their mission. Nahum hoped their agent had located the crate containing the ACTEN chips.

The number of outsiders involved in their plans was another point of contention for Nahum. However, he would be in complete control once he took custody of the American technology. He had total authority in Jurre's absence, although it wasn't as if he needed it. His troops were as loyal to him as they were to Jurre; the Kahane Chai brotherhood demanded strict obedience. Nonetheless, respect was something earned by men when led with a balance of authority and loyalty.

Nahum took care of his men and they took care of him. Simple.

A Hummer painted olive drab pulled up, and the driver smiled. Nahum returned the smile as he climbed into the vehicle.

"It is time for our revenge, sir," the young man said.

Nahum clapped his Kahane brother on the shoulder.

"Vengeance is God's alone, Mikael," he replied, "and we are simply the tools of that vengeance. You must never forget this."

Mikael cast a forlorn expression and lowered his eyes, a submissive gesture out of respect for his older and more learned superior. Nahum understood Mikael's excitement. The intensity among the Kahane soldiers was obvious. They were ready for this operation—they had trained many months for it. When the time came, they would perform their duties without question.

Finally, they would devour their enemy.

AN MP WAVED Mack Bolan's government sedan through the front gates of Fort Carson.

Bolan returned the soldier's salute as he drove past, then continued along the main road. The weather had cleared during Bolan's seventy-mile drive to Colorado Springs. The sun beat through the windows of the sedan and glinted off the silver eagles on the epaulettes of Bolan's dress uniform. The soldier adjusted the air conditioner to high and followed the map provided by Stony Man.

Lieutenant Colonel Jacoby's office was in a two-story brick building nestled among a row of identical structures that were centrally located on Fort Carson. Bolan parked in a lot across the street, snatched the briefcase next to him and exited his sedan.

As he walked toward the building marked Special Detachments, Bolan returned a score of salutes from soldiers along the sidewalk. Appearances were everything, and Bolan felt right at home in a military setting. Protocol would have required him to report to the post commander first, but there would be time for that later. He wanted to get his hands dirty—find out more about Jacoby's operation.

According to Stony Man intelligence, Jacoby was in command of about thirty or forty troops for the escort operation. Stony Man had also forwarded information about the post. Officially activated during World War II, Fort Carson occupied more than forty thousand acres. The Third Brigade Combat Team—the Iron Brigade—was one of the largest units on the post. It included armor, field artillery, infantry and engineer battalions. Two other units were attached to the Third

BCT: Charlie Company, 104th MI and a signal company of the 534th SIG.

As Bolan neared the building, his eye caught the familiar outlines of armor moving along a distant track trail. The soldier recognized many of the vehicles. Three M2A2 Bradley Fighting Vehicles led a group of M1A1 Abrams and M109A6 155 mm Paladins. Dust was churned up as the heavy armor wove its path toward South Range. Bolan surmised they were headed out for maneuvers.

Like many U.S. installations, the Mountain Post prided itself on maintaining a high degree of combat readiness. The Third BCT was a subunit of the 104th Infantry Division at Fort Hood, Texas, the largest armor-equipped installation in the free world.

The sight of U.S. military might was still impressive.

Bolan found Jacoby's office on the first floor. The small cubicle occupied a space outside the office door. A young blond specialist in camouflage BDUs snapped to attention as Bolan entered the office and whipped a salute that the Executioner returned tiredly.

"May I help you, sir?"

"Colonel Pollock to see Lieutenant Colonel Jacoby," Bolan replied. "I believe he's expecting me."

"Certainly, sir."

The soldier turned and knocked on Jacoby's door, waiting for a reply before he opened it and walked inside. Bolan followed the specialist without waiting, and moved with the impertinence and self-importance that typified the trained bureaucrat.

"Sir—" the young man began.

"Colonel Rance Pollock," Bolan interrupted. "I'm attaché to Chairman of the Senate Arms Committee."

The man seated behind his desk immediately rose and saluted, but Bolan noticed he was under Jacoby's scrutiny. Military courtesy was the soldier's only advantage. He outranked Jacoby, but it was obvious he wasn't welcome.

Jacoby dropped the salute, then dismissed his aide. When the specialist was gone, Jacoby rose from his chair and indicated for Bolan to have a seat. He came around the desk and offered his hand, which the Executioner shook limply. Jacoby was tall, with salt-and-pepper hair and a muscular physique. He wore camouflage BDUs, as well, but there was a bit more to the uniform. The lightning patch with Special Forces rocker covered his left shoulder, and there were two combat patches on his right sleeve. Over his left chest Bolan identified the airborne, air-assault and combat-infantry-badge insignia. A cluster in subdued black ran along the length of his right collar.

Bolan sat stiffly, crossing his legs as Jacoby returned to the chair behind his desk.

"I'll cut right to the chase, sir," Jacoby said flatly. "I don't agree with your presence here. This is a sensitive operation."

"I can sympathize with that, Colonel," Bolan said.

"Washington has made it clear I'm to cooperate with you and to answer any questions that you may have. I've got no beef with that, okay?"

Bolan nodded.

"However," Jacoby continued, not missing a beat, "my first mission is to guarantee that this operation goes smoothly. I call the shots…period. Do we understand each other, sir?"

Bolan fixed Jacoby with a cold blue gaze and an icy smile.

"I'm not here to call the shots, Jacoby," Bolan replied. "I'm simply here to assist and observe. That's the extent of it. The results will speak for themselves where the Senate Arms Committee is concerned."

Bolan tried to remain cool as Jacoby stared at him. He could practically see the wheels turning. The man was trying to decide if Bolan was being genuine or insolent. Bolan could feel for Jacoby's predicament. The man had an important mission, and he didn't need some Washington boy wonder breathing down his neck.

Nevertheless, Bolan wasn't going to back down.

Jacoby sat back in his chair and grunted. The tone of his voice became more casual.

"I have to admit, you're not what I expected." He nodded at Bolan's numerous citations. "You've been around awhile."

"I've seen my share. I came out of the Gulf on an extended medical. Took enough shrapnel to build a tank. When I was well enough, they kicked me to a desk job."

"Refused to a Combat Arms MOS, eh?"

"Strictly administrative now." Bolan gestured to his lapel. "This is probably the highest rank I'll ever see in this field."

"That's too bad, sir," Jacoby replied genuinely. "There don't seem to be too many of us war horses left. I've been lucky, I guess."

Bolan simply nodded.

"Okay," Jacoby continued, "what would you like to know?"

"Just the basics. How is training proceeding?"

"I think it's gone well. The complement for the actual operation will be thirty-four, including myself. I didn't get a choice in the selection process. Training these guys hasn't been an easy task, sir."

"I don't imagine," Bolan replied. "How does that number break down?"

"Twenty-four comprise two teams from the Tenth Special Forces Group. Team Alpha will be the primary, and Bravo will handle backup and support. The remaining are either signal or linguistics experts, and four combat engineers to handle the mobility and equipment issues."

"Do you have an executive officer?"

"Yes, sir. Captain Ralston is my XO. He has a background in military intelligence."

"Did you choose him, or was he assigned, as well?" Bolan pressed.

"No, sir, he was selected by Department of the Army," Jacoby said abruptly. "Ralston's a smart one. College grad from West Point, and another two years of training for his position in MI. From what I know, he doesn't have a lick of combat experience. Between ourselves, I've never been much for the MI boys.''

Bolan smiled and nodded as if in agreement. He was happy with the news of the breakdown. He knew the Mossad agent wasn't among the combat teams, so he could exclude the officers, the two SF teams and the combat engineers. That left only four possible candidates, so identification probably wouldn't be tough. Bolan carefully considered the information before he posed his next question.

''When will your unit leave for Israel?''

''Sorry, sir,'' Jacoby replied quietly, ''but that's need-to-know. I can say we're on a tight schedule and I wouldn't get too comfortable.''

''Fair enough,'' Bolan said easily. ''May I see the training area?''

''No problem.'' Jacoby rose from his chair and snatched his beret from a nearby rack. ''The training area is completely sealed off from outside personnel, but your quarters are housed with ours. If you need to make any phone calls, you must do it now. Once inside the training area, you'll be there until we leave.''

''That won't be necessary,'' Bolan said quickly.

The men left the building by a back exit that opened onto a small motor pool. Jacoby led Bolan to a Hummer with its roof removed. He drove them onto the main road and headed south. After a few minutes, they turned and followed a track trail.

Bolan kept himself orientated, memorizing the lay of the land. Jacoby drove the dusty trail west toward rolling foothills. The landscape of dark reds and browns was dotted with flecks of light green foliage and the gray-white of sagebrush. Jacoby slowed the Hummer and made a sudden sharp turn just past a rise in the trail.

''It seems strange that they would use that many personnel for this kind of sensitive operation,'' Bolan ventured.

Jacoby shrugged as he replied, "The numbers *are* a little high, but I can manage it. Most of the spec ops I've done used one SF team, which is a standard complement of twelve."

Mack Bolan smiled. He had evidently maintained his cover. The Executioner knew exactly how many soldiers made up a Special Forces team. He knew what the individual duties were of each member, how they operated and just about everything else there was to know.

"I can understand the need for backup," Bolan said.

"Yes, sir. I guess it's obvious," Jacoby answered matter-of-factly. "We're touching down in a small village outside of Jerusalem. Total operation time is thirty minutes, so enter the added hands. I could have pulled this off with one team and four engineers, but my superiors insisted on a spare team and the people from MI."

They approached a gate guarded by four Green Berets toting M-16 A-2 rifles. The gate was a square steel frame meshed with barbed wire in a crisscross pattern. A triple cyclone fence of two side-by-side concertina rolls topped by a third, branched from the gate in either direction. A roll extended forty-five feet and was secured with metal wires to pickets spaced at fifteen-foot intervals. The fence circled the perimeter, which Bolan guessed covered at least a thousand square yards.

Bolan's eye caught the structures inside the compound. The mock Israeli village was visible through the fence. He had been to Israel many times, and he was impressed with the accuracy of the construction. The village was designed with every last detail in place. Sand had been poured to simulate the arid desert, and it was an odd sight, considering the cool breeze that rolled off the mountainside.

Jacoby brought the Hummer to a grinding halt and returned the salutes of his men. He jerked a thumb in Bolan's direction and ordered them to log the new arrival. The Executioner mechanically recited his name, rank and service number. One of the soldiers moved the gate aside after an exchange of passwords. Bolan didn't bother to memorize the information. He wouldn't be leaving until the mission was under way, and the password would likely change at midnight.

Jacoby parked the Hummer in front of the mock village. Bolan exited and stretched as he took in the village houses. It was uncanny—everything was in its place. The buildings were built with real mud bricks and sandstone; there were no synthetics. Wooden beams protruded from below the rooflines, and the square windows were blocked with straw shades. Heavy doors of raw wood attached by cheap hinges blocked the entrances to outside elements.

Jacoby stood patiently and waited for Bolan to take it in before leading the way past the small houses into the courtyard formed by the circular layout of the houses. A well and cistern occupied the center of the courtyard, shaded by decorative canvas sheets mounted on cedar poles.

In a true Israeli village, this would have been the public area.

"Impressive," Bolan finally said. He looked at Jacoby, adding, "Where are the troops?"

Jacoby checked his watch. "They're probably still at the firing range. If you'll follow me, sir, your quarters are this way."

Bolan followed Jacoby through the mock-up and they emerged on the other side. The barracks were actually four Quonset huts. Two served as barracks for the troops, a third for the MI and signal people, and one hut was set up perpendicular to the other three. That was the officers' quarters, and Jacoby led Bolan inside to a small cubicle in back. Bolan's quarters had been hastily furnished with a bunk, a small lamp, a desk and a chair. A large duffel bag lay on the bed.

"They sent your equipment ahead of time," Jacoby explained. "I don't think Class As will get you through the next few days." He pointed to a door on the far side of the tin building. "Latrine and shower is through there. The other huts aren't equipped with electricity or running water. I didn't want them to have anything they weren't going to have on the mission."

"Makes sense," Bolan agreed. "It sounds like you have the situation well in hand, Colonel."

Jacoby didn't appear overly moved by the compliment.

"I'll leave you to get settled, sir," Jacoby said. "At about 1700 hours, the troops will be back. We have a training scenario set up for 1730. You're welcome to observe, sir. I'll send Captain Ralston when we're ready to commence."

Once Jacoby had left, Bolan wasted no time in trading his dress uniform for fatigues and polished combat boots. Bolan quickly checked the bag and found his .44 Desert Eagle buried between spare sets of fatigues along with two spare clips. There was also a set of load-bearing equipment suspenders attached to a pistol belt with a flap holster. A combat knife was secured in a quick-release sheath that hung vertically on one of the suspenders, its handle pointing downward. A crook-neck flashlight was attached to the other suspender.

The Executioner smiled at that—Brognola never missed a beat.

Bolan holstered the Eagle in place, hung the LBE on the metal rail of his bunk and tossed the duffel bag underneath. He pulled his Beretta from the briefcase he'd brought and concealed it in the cargo pocket of his trousers.

Bolan looked forward to meeting the rest of the escort team. He also considered the new problem of no communications. He could operate on his own, but the President would probably demand constant reports. The safe delivery of these chips was too important, and Bolan would have no contact with Stony Man. He would have to find some way of getting intelligence out when the time came.

As Bolan lay back on his bunk, he began to concentrate on the immediate task of locating the Mossad agent. Four possibilities were hardly an insurmountable task. If the agent was a native of Israel, even with training in American language and dress, there were ethnic features that couldn't be disguised. Once he'd made the identification, Bolan would get the full story.

The soldier closed his eyes to rest. For now, all he could do was wait.

4

The sound of movement immediately woke Bolan.

"Good afternoon, sir."

A fresh-faced man stood over him. Subdued twin bars were sewn to the collar of his BDU blouse. He was younger than Bolan expected, maybe thirty, with bright blue eyes and short blond hair. He had a pencil-thin mustache, and wrinkles appeared at the corners of his eyes when he smiled.

Bolan immediately sat up from his bunk.

"I'm Captain Ralston, sir," the man said, saluting.

"At ease, Captain," Bolan replied, returning Ralston's salute.

He offered his hand and Ralston shook it enthusiastically.

"Colonel Jacoby asked me to escort you to the training demonstration, sir."

Bolan rose and found he towered over Ralston. The guy was short—probably just met the Army's minimum-height requirement for males. There was something intent and exciting in Ralston's mannerisms, as if he were on speed or something. The effect was both impressive and irritating, and Bolan could see why a guy like Jacoby wasn't overly thrilled with his executive officer.

"Lead the way, Captain," Bolan said, donning his BDU cap and LBE harness.

Bolan followed Ralston out of the hut and around the outside of the village houses until they reached one house with steps built into the back. A small dais at the top supported two chairs and a field table with binoculars. The added height afforded a perfect view of the entire compound.

From his vantage point, Bolan could make out another Quonset hut in the distance. An M2A2 Bradley sat in front of the hut. Bolan wondered what was inside. Jacoby hadn't mentioned anything about taking heavy armor for their mission.

About twenty yards from the village, Bolan also saw a mock-up of the rear half of a C-141 cargo plane. It was probably identical to the type of plane that would be used to transport the chips. The chips would obviously have to be airlifted into the country.

Ralston made sure Bolan was comfortable and then excused himself. Within a few minutes, he saw Ralston as the man joined Jacoby and the rest of the team below. He had a brief conversation with the SF colonel before the teams split up, one heading for the houses while the other disappeared inside the mock plane.

Bolan heard a whistle sound twice, and the action was under way. Six Green Berets cradling M-16s appeared from the back of the C-141 and fanned out in a semicircle. They fell prone to the ground and pointed their weapons toward assigned fields of fire. Moments later, six more SF commandos exited the plane hatch, escorting a large unmarked crate on a hydraulic lift operated by two combat engineers.

Two more engineers took up positions ahead of the escort team. They wore full Kevlar body armor and carried mine detectors. Colonel Jacoby and Captain Ralston then appeared, accompanied by a female soldier who carried a backpack with protruding antennae.

As the crate was brought toward the village, a weird silence fell over the entire area. It was as if time had stood still, and even Bolan could feel the anticipation of the soldiers.

Sand and dirt suddenly erupted to the left of the group. The hydraulic operators immediately whirled and headed back to the plane. The Green Berets holding rear echelon surrounded the crate and provided covering fire. The six SF commandos on point jumped to their feet and began a fire-and-maneuver pattern toward the village as more explosions ensued.

Automatic weapons opened up from the village perimeter. The first thing Bolan noticed was the odd sound of the weapons fire. It wasn't the sound of M-16 rifles, but rather the unmistakable rattle of Uzis.

An explosion lifted one Green Beret off his feet.

Bolan watched with shock as the man's arm separated from the rest of his body and flew in an opposite direction. The man landed hard, his screams obvious in the magnified view through the binoculars. The sound was drowned out by the "mock" explosions around him.

A second soldier quickly met the same fate.

Bolan was off the dais and down the steps of the observation tower in seconds. The Beretta was clutched in his fist as he ran through the village courtyard. He sprinted for one of the makeshift Israeli houses on the far side. His ears rang with small-arms fire as he crashed through the door of the house and swept the interior.

Two men in desert fatigues were set up near an open window. Their Uzis protruded around the straw-mat coverings, and they were laying down a continuous barrage of fire. One of the men turned to face Bolan, a look of surprise spreading across his face. The man pulled his Uzi from the window and started to stand as he swung the muzzle toward Bolan.

The Executioner was ready.

Bolan thumbed the selector to 3-round bursts and stroked the trigger. The 9 mm Parabellum rounds ripped through the gunman's chest and head. The impact caused him to twist and tumble into his partner, who was unaware Bolan had entered the house.

The second gunman pushed at the weight of his cohort with an aggravated grunt, and his eyes widened when he saw the Executioner's shadowy form. A pair of cold blue eyes stared at the man above the gaping barrel of the Beretta.

The gunman began to curse in Hebrew, bringing up his Uzi.

Bolan fired another 3-round burst, the rounds stitching an ugly pattern across the man's chest. Frothy red sputum flecked the gunman's lips and chin as the Parabellum shockers slammed him against the wall below the window. The man slid to the ground at an awkward angle and let out a dying gasp before he lay still.

Bolan noticed a dark pile in one corner of the house. It was the two friendlies, SF commandos who had been part of the original assault team. Bolan moved toward them for a closer look. Blood caked their shirts where it had run freely from gaping incisions in their necks. They had been garroted.

A fresh cluster of explosions jarred the Executioner. They were closer this time, and the concussions rocked the foundation of the small building. Dust rained from the ceiling as Bolan pocketed the Beretta and scooped up the two Uzis. He moved to the front door of the house and opened it enough to visualize the scene before him.

It was a horrific sight.

Four more SF commandos had fallen under Uzi fire. The remaining eight Green Berets were huddled behind the crate with the two officers, the engineers and the woman soldier with the radio. Jacoby had his side arm out and was returning fire. Bolan stepped out the doorway and motioned them to come toward him. The woman spotted the Executioner first. She turned to Ralston and pointed in Bolan's direction.

Bolan turned the Uzis on the neighboring house. The weapons chattered in unison as he provided covering fire. A burst of 9 mm rounds peppered the exterior, churning up clouds of dust and debris. Two Green Berets fell under fire from the unseen enemy, and Ralston tripped and fell. Before the MI officer could rise, a grenade sailed through the air and landed near him. The subsequent explosion tore Ralston to shreds.

The remainder of Jacoby's group sprinted for the house. Bolan continued the firestorm, alternating his bursts and directing fire at any movement inside the neighboring houses.

The soldiers pushed past Bolan and crashed through the door as one of the Uzis died in the warrior's hand.

The bolt locked back.

Bolan stepped through the doorway and slammed it shut. The house was cloaked in darkness. The weapons fire and explosions ceased, and the only sounds were the labored breathing of the group. The stillness was eerie.

"Keep down," Bolan ordered them.

The Executioner crouched and moved to Jacoby's position near the window. He quickly stripped the men he'd killed of their extra magazines. He loaded one Uzi and handed it to Jacoby, then loaded the second one and kept it for himself.

"What the hell just happened, sir?" Jacoby asked in horror.

"I wish I knew," Bolan snapped. He looked around the room. "Is anybody else armed?"

Bravo Team's CO, Lieutenant Nick Ford, duckwalked over to the trio. "We've got rifles, sir, but no live rounds."

Bolan nodded grimly. "Great."

"Th-this is insane," Jacoby stammered. "There are a half-dozen dead men out there!"

"How many were part of your assault team, Colonel?" Bolan asked.

"Ten," Jacoby said immediately. "All from Team Alpha, less two assigned to guard the front gates."

"Minus these two," Bolan said, gesturing to the bodies, "that brings the count to at least six. I think it's safe to at least double that number."

"Terrorists?" the woman soldier asked.

"Probably," Bolan replied, looking at her with some surprise.

It appeared he had found the Mossad agent.

"Terrorists?" Jacoby reiterated. "What the hell are you two talking about?"

"But how did they get inside?" the woman continued, ignoring Jacoby's question.

"Slipped in during the night, I'm sure," Bolan said.

"What the hell is going on, sir?" Jacoby demanded.

Bolan scowled. "Obviously, somebody intends to steal those chips. That was Uzi fire you were taking out there."

"Where did they get Uzis?"

"Look, Jacoby, I don't have time to explain. We need to come up with a plan to get out of here."

A mixture of surprise and realization spread across Jacoby's face as he stared at Bolan. "I have the feeling you're not from the Senate Arms Committee. Are you?"

"Not even close," the Executioner replied.

THE SUN WAS SETTING behind the distant mountains when Major General Donald Wasserman briskly entered the offices of post headquarters.

There was a flurry of activity in the building. Soldiers in full combat gear moved through the building. Civilian firefighters were already on scene, under heavy escort by MPs. The building was dark. All electrical power was gone, the computer screens were black, and Wasserman's harried staff was desperately trying to call public utilities and support companies. Untold pandemonium had erupted, and nobody seemed to have any answers.

Second Lieutenant Cynthia Asher was the general's personal secretary. Her normal, rocklike composure was gone. She had obviously dressed in a hurry—her Class A uniform was rumpled, her hair pulled up loosely, and she didn't wear a trace of makeup. She rushed to Wasserman's side, struggling to keep pace with her commanding officer as he strolled into his office.

"Report," Wasserman snapped.

"We have no idea what's going on, sir," Asher said mechanically. "The entire post just shut down. We have no electrical systems, backup generators have failed and the entire computer network is down."

Wasserman waved at the telephone on his desk. "The phone systems aren't working, either?"

"None of them, sir," Asher replied. "We have engineers here now trying to hook up field lines."

"Where's Major Dunham?"

Malcolm Dunham was Fort Carson's executive officer, and Wasserman's most trusted aide. Wasserman had personally selected Dunham to serve as his XO. He was calm under fire and a model soldier in every sense of the word. Wasserman could hardly believe Dunham wasn't present in such an emergency. He needed to find the man and get a better feel for the present situation.

"He's roving the post now, sir," Asher said. "He took a group from the Third BCT, and they're surveying the area to see what's needed. He's already declared a post-wide emergency under your authority."

"He's a good man," Wasserman said calmly. "Do we have any idea what could have caused this yet, Lieutenant?"

"Not yet, sir. We're still trying to piece together the extent of the problem."

"I'd say the problem is pretty obvious already."

"Yes, sir."

Wasserman sat at his desk and leaned back in his chair. He needed a moment to address the situation. Such an enormous shutdown could only be caused by some kind of computer glitch. What disturbed him most was that backup systems weren't operable. It could have been a virus, possibly even an outside act of aggression.

The situation was frustrating.

Wasserman came from the school of hard knocks. He was a twenty-five-year career soldier, a graduate of West Point and the War College. He had started as a young second lieutenant with an infantry company in Vietnam. From there, he had served in other divisions on multiple continents. His experience and leadership abilities had finally landed him a job as post commander at Fort Devons, Massachusetts. When Devons closed, he was promoted to major general and assigned to Fort Carson.

Wasserman's experiences told him that one had to be able to identify an enemy before one could fight it. However, there was no enemy to identify here. A systems-wide failure was very odd indeed, and there weren't many alternatives. Fort Carson served the civilian population of Colorado Springs and El Paso County as much as their own troops. It wasn't safe to resume normal operations until they had the situation under control. It was time to consult his higher-ups. However, he needed to take decisive action for the duration of the emergency.

"Lieutenant, I want every unit on full alert. No one is to leave this compound, and no one is to enter unless personally approved by either me or Major Dunham."

"Understood, sir." Asher turned to leave, then whirled to face Wasserman on afterthought. "What about the civilian employees, sir?"

"Begin immediate evacuation of all civilian workers who haven't already left for the day," Wasserman ordered. "And make it clear I do *not* want them talking to the press."

"You know that's going to be difficult, sir."

"I don't care, Lieutenant. Just tell them what I said. Now you have your orders, so get moving."

"Yes, sir."

As Asher left the room and headed down the hallway, Wasserman called after her, "And find me Colonel Jacoby!"

"JACOBY, WHAT'S IN that hut by the Bradley?" Mack Bolan asked.

"We're using it for a garage," Jacoby replied. "All we have in there are a few five-ton trucks."

"And the chips," the Mossad woman supplied.

Jacoby fired a harsh stare at her, which she appeared to ignore.

"You must be my contact," Bolan said.

"My name is Ilia Yasso," she replied with a nod.

She leaned forward and ripped open the fatigue shirt of one

of the men Bolan had killed. A strange symbol was burned into the man's chest, its image permanently engraved there by scar tissue.

"I know this mark," Yasso said. "These men are Kahane Chai."

"That explains some things," Bolan said with a nod.

He handed her his Uzi. "I think you know how to use this, then."

"Of course." Yasso took the weapon and professionally yanked the charging handle to chamber a round from the fresh magazine.

"I'm not even going to ask what's going on here," Jacoby muttered.

"Good," Bolan snapped, "because we don't have that kind of time." He looked around and then fixed the SF leader with a hard stare. "Your first concern will be to get your men out of here."

"What are you planning to do, sir?"

"Provide a diversion. I want you to split the remainder of this group into three-man teams. When I go out the door, get to the main post and get help."

"What about the chips?" Jacoby asked.

"You worry about getting your people out. I'll take care of the chips."

Although everyone present was a soldier, Bolan couldn't risk their assistance. There was a difference between dying in the line of duty and dying needlessly. The Kahane Chai terrorists were highly trained and very dangerous. Their mission would be of paramount concern. They didn't really care how many people they had to kill, and had already proved they would murder unarmed soldiers without provocation.

The Executioner didn't intend to sacrifice any more lives.

Bolan gave a quick nod to the group and then burst through the front door, the .44 Desert Eagle in one fist and Beretta in the other. He triggered his pistols on the surrounding houses, and a maelstrom of gunfire responded to the challenge. Bolan made a beeline to the crate and dived for cover. He could hear the Uzi rounds strike the front of the crate. More 9 mm slugs chewed up the sand around him.

Bolan peered around the bottom edge and saw one Uzi gunner partially visible inside one of the houses. He swung the Beretta around the corner and triggered a 3-round burst. The terrorist's head snapped backward and he disappeared into the darkness. Chalk up one more for the Green Berets who lay dead around Bolan.

Soon, the count would be even.

Bolan left his cover and sprinted toward the Quonset hut in the distance. A fresh eruption of gunfire threatened to overtake him, but he made it past the plane mock-up. As Bolan continued to close the gap, the outline of the Bradley became clearer. It had been some time since he had driven the armored fighting vehicle, but that wouldn't pose a serious problem.

Military vehicles were actually designed to be easy to handle. The Army didn't want to make teaching new soldiers how to drive their equipment a complicated process. Valuable time would be wasted in AIT courses if vehicle operators needed long hours to train. Any basic soldier had to be able to drive equipment. In combat, there wasn't time for thorough driving instruction, so most soldiers were mandated to at least know how to operate wheeled vehicles.

Mack Bolan's experience went far beyond that.

The Executioner mounted the armored vehicle and climbed through the driver's hatch. The M2A2 Bradley was a work of modern military art as much as armored hardware. It was more than twenty-one feet in length, weighed close to thirty-three tons and could travel forty-five miles per hour. It was armored with a Kevlar spall liner under 5083-series aluminum and homogenous steel plating. Its armament included a 25 mm M242 Bushmaster chain gun as a primary weapon, and a 7.62 mm M240C coaxial machine gun.

The normal complement included a gunner, driver and track commander. Bolan couldn't drive and shoot effectively on his own, but then he wouldn't have to. The very presence of the Bradley would more than even the odds. As he keyed the ignition and the Cummins six-hundred-horsepower engine roared in his ears, Bolan knew he was about to change the course of the battle.

It was time to fight fire with firepower.

The Executioner rolled across the compound and stopped the Bradley near the mock C-141. He abandoned the driver's seat for the gunnery chair, and pressed his eye to the thermal-imaging day sight. The targets were easy enough to acquire magnified at four times their size. Bolan could place the armor-piercing rounds from the Bushmaster with accuracy and effect.

That would flush the rabbits from their holes.

The soldier kicked up the engine power and brought all systems online as he acquired the first target. A green flashing in the scope indicated an "all-go" condition, and Bolan opened fire. The Bushmaster spit AP rounds at a rate of two hundred per minute through the windows of the houses.

Bolan swept the village perimeter with the gun turret. Huge chunks of plaster and stone exploded from the house exteriors and rained on the score of terrorists now scrambling from their cover. Some of the AP rounds struck flesh, tearing bodies apart like tigers shredding their prey.

Bolan's viewfinder settled onto one Kahane terrorist. The Executioner watched the man drop to one knee and sight on the Bradley with an M-72A2 LAW. The special Applique armor tile system had been added to the M2A2 models with the idea of defeating ballistic ammunition and increasing protection against shaped-charge weapons. However, the LAW was more than capable of immobilizing the Bradley.

Bolan triggered the chain gun a second after he saw the flash from the LAW's gaping opening. He pried himself from the seat and bailed for the top hatch. The HE round exploded as the soldier reached it. A violent concussion shook the ground, and he could feel the heat as it pierced his armored cocoon. The blast caused him to lose his balance and slammed him against the back of the driver's headrest.

Blood gushed from a large gash in the Executioner's forehead.

He fought back the inky blackness that threatened to overtake him.

5

Jacoby, Yasso and the rest of the team burst through the back door of the house as soon as Bolan left.

Yasso fell into step behind Jacoby, who handed his pistol to Lieutenant Ford.

"Take your men and find an alternate way to the Quonset hut. Protect those chips at any cost. You hear me?" Jacoby demanded.

"Yes, sir," Ford replied.

"You," Jacoby said, pointing to Yasso, "stay with me."

"Colonel Pollock told us to—"

"I don't give a damn what Pollock said, lady," Jacoby shot back, heading in the direction of the nearby Quonset huts. "This is *my* operation, you got that?"

Yasso followed him but watched for the appearance of Kahane Chai soldiers. They made it to the officers' hut without incident. Yasso took a position near the front doors and covered the entrance with the Uzi.

Jacoby ran to his desk and wound the ringer handle on a field phone.

"Hello?" Jacoby cursed under his breath as he wound the telephone again. "Does anybody copy?"

Yasso wasn't surprised at the lack of reply. Their chances of leaving alive were slim. With the Kahane Chai swarming the compound, there would be more trouble before all was said and done. Yasso was quite familiar with the capabilities of her fellow Jews.

While the Kach and Kahane Chai weren't nearly as fanatical as the Palestinians were, they were twice as dangerous. They had supporters everywhere. Many of those who backed their movement could probably be found right here in America. The Anti-Defamation League and other Semitic organizations among the Jewish populations felt a growing urgency in the Kach-Kahane Chai mission.

It seemed to Yasso that the restoration of her people as a nation had created more problems than solutions. The Middle East was a central forum for terrorism, violence and war. Corrupt leaders had spawned a horrible creature. No single entity, not even the Mossad or Israel Defense Forces, could combat the catastrophe of the terror machine. It had spread its ugly tentacles across a nation already subjected to dissension and anarchy.

Nonetheless, a select few had taken up arms to answer the call of freedom. In that moment, Yasso was comforted only by the thought of a certain dark-haired, blue-eyed stranger who was fighting for those rare reasons such as duty, honor and country. Somewhere out there, the man called Pollock was risking his life to make a difference for Yasso and her people.

She could only respect him for that.

"Dammit, the lines are dead!" Jacoby called.

"Probably cut, Colonel," Yasso responded, not taking her eyes from the front door.

Two dark-skinned men in camouflage and carrying Uzis suddenly burst through the door, their weapons sweeping the room.

Her training took over as Yasso dropped to one knee, sighted down the barrel, took a deep breath and squeezed the trigger. The weapon rattled in her fists as a trio of 9 mm Parabellum shockers punched holes in the nearer invader's chest. The man did a pirouette, his eyes going wide as he fell through the doorway.

The second gunman tripped on his partner. He recovered his balance but not in time. Yasso fired two short bursts that smashed into the terrorist's face. Blood and brain matter flew in all directions as the nearly headless corpse dropped to the floor like a stone.

Yasso turned to see Jacoby staring at her with a shocked expression.

"Where the hell did you learn how to shoot like that?"

"Basic training, sir," Yasso muttered.

She rushed to the bodies and stripped them of their weapons, handing both Uzis to Jacoby. Yasso requested Jacoby assist her with sliding the load-bearing suspenders from the deceased pair. M-33 fragmentation grenades hung from the suspenders, and there were Jericho pistols in holsters on the pistol belts.

"We'd better get out of here, Colonel," Yasso suggested.

Jacoby nodded, and they checked the village perimeter before leaving the hut. Yasso considered their new situation. Pollock hadn't offered a contingency plan for this new turn of events. It was a long way to the perimeter fence in any direction. They had no way to cut through the fence even if they made it. With any luck, one of Ford's teams had already escaped.

It wouldn't be too long before help arrived.

Yasso led Jacoby to an empty house nearby and the two huddled in the darkness.

"What are you planning to do?" Yasso asked him.

"Just let me think a second," Jacoby snapped.

Moments elapsed before gunfire could be heard. It was the sound of heavy weapons coming from the direction of the enemy position. Yasso smiled. It sounded as if Pollock had kept his promise.

"I think our best bet would be to try for that front gate," Jacoby finally said. "Do you feel up to it?"

"You're in charge, Colonel."

"Then let's move out."

They left the house and ran through the village courtyard. Before they could reach the other side, four Kahane terrorists poured from the rear door of a house to their left. Their Uzis were aimed in Jacoby and Yasso's direction. The pair split off, Yasso rushing for cover behind one of the houses while Jacoby continued out of the courtyard.

Yasso realized Jacoby hadn't noticed the enemy in his haste to escape. Before she could sound a warning, the quartet of Kahane soldiers opened fire on her and Jacoby's positions. The SF colonel was cut down in a hail of shots. The rounds ripped through his arms and legs, and drilled angry holes into his back and head.

Jacoby's flesh seemed to explode from his body as he flew into a nearby door face first. He bounced off and fell onto his back, leaving a bloody impression on the door.

Yasso screamed in fury as she steadied her captured Uzi in a two-handed grip. She lay prone on the sunbaked sand, bracing the Uzi with her elbows, and squeezed the trigger, coaxing short but controlled bursts from the chattering Israeli weapon.

The Kahane Chai terrorists tried to spread out as their first man fell under Yasso's deadly resolve. An S pattern of red holes spread across the gunman's belly and chest. His body flipped into the air at an awkward angle.

Yasso had already acquired her next target before the first terrorist hit the ground in a cloud of dust. Her shot pattern was tight with a sustained burst. Most of the concentrated force of the rounds nearly decapitated the Kahane soldier. He staggered aimlessly a moment before collapsing to the ground.

Another gunner had lined up a clear shot on Yasso's position. She saw the threat and rolled away from her cover as the enemy soldier triggered his weapon. The Parabellum rounds chewed up the space the woman had occupied a moment before. One bullet ricocheted off a large rock near the house, and a fragment caught Yasso under her right eye. She blinked back the pain and struggled to maintain her concentration over the sensation of blood running down her cheek.

Yasso came out of the roll on her knees and fired another burst from the Uzi. Bullets slammed into her opponent's chest and drove him back. The man's rearward motion was caught up short by the well in the center of the courtyard. His body flipped over the edge and disappeared into the darkness.

Yasso felt something violently jar her chin and hands. She looked down to see the Uzi had been shot from her grip. The rear sight of the weapon had cut a neat furrow in the soft tissue under her jaw. She quickly reached for the Jericho pistol, but stopped when she noticed the fourth Kahane terrorist had her covered.

His bronze skin was masked by a sheen of sweat. Daylight glinted in his dark eyes and his lips curled back to reveal a row of stark white teeth. It was odd to see one of her own countrymen dressed in the uniform of a U.S. Special Forces commando. Actually, Yasso rescinded that idea—the man was a traitor not a brother. He had allied himself with everything she hated.

"Get up!" he ordered her in Hebrew.

Yasso rose and raised her hands above her head. It was wiser to do just what the man commanded. He wouldn't hesitate to shoot her if she got out of line. It was more than just being a soldier. It had to do with being a man. In Israel, most women were considered second-class citizens. It was the nature of their society. Having spent considerable time in America, Yasso would probably never be able to accept the position of an underling.

The Kahane terrorist ordered her to turn around, and then expertly frisked her and secured the weapons. He commanded her to strip the LBE suspenders and belt, and then shoved his Uzi into the small of her back. He prodded her in the direction of the Quonset huts.

Abruptly, the fresh sounds of small arms echoed in Yasso's ears.

It seemed Pollock was alive and well.

BLOOD STUNG ONE of Mack Bolan's eyes as it ran down his face.

He wiped it away with irritation and rose to a sitting position. He was angry with himself. It wasn't typical for the soldier to put himself in such a precarious position. Stupid mistakes were what could get a warrior killed fast, and Bolan made as few as possible. Nevertheless, his experience had led him to conclude he wasn't superhuman, and mistakes were part of the game.

Bolan had learned to accept them from himself now and again.

The Executioner drew a combat knife from his belt and tore two strips of cloth from his fatigue shirt. He bunched one, pressed it against the wound, then tied the other one around his head.

Bolan struggled to find the light switch in the dark interior of the Bradley. He finally located the lever and twisted it in a circular motion. Nothing happened. Bolan flipped the switch again, but the familiar array of lights didn't appear and the targeting system refused to light up.

The explosion had probably fried the batteries.

The sound of boots walking on top of the tank reached the Executioner's ears. The head injury had to have been more serious than Bolan had originally anticipated, because those faint noises thundered inside his skull. He reached into his cargo pocket and withdrew the Beretta.

Bolan flicked the selector switch to single-shot mode.

Sunlight nearly blinded him as the TC hatch fell back and two Kahane terrorists peered into the hole.

The soldier took both terrorists with well-placed shots to the heads. One fell away from the hatch opening as the other dropped into it. The Kahane terrorist's Uzi clattered to the deck plates.

Bolan snatched the weapon and scrambled to the rear hatch.

A group of six terrorists had formed a semicircle around the front of the tank. None of them appeared to be expecting the Executioner as he emerged from the rear of his dead vehicle. Bolan used the surprise to his advantage. He dropped to the ground and rolled away from the Bradley, triggering his Uzi on the move. The Israeli machine pistol vibrated in his fists as the soldier sprayed the men who were foolishly clustered together.

The Uzi chattered mercilessly and dropped one Kahane soldier after another. Several of the enemy appeared to dance before they collapsed under the hail of autofire. Rounds ripped through their bellies, chests and heads, and pools of blood were quickly soaked up by the sunbaked sands that had been poured there by human hands.

When the last terrorist had fallen, Bolan got to one knee and swept the area with the muzzle of the Uzi. He could hear more Uzi fire in the distance, but no resistance appeared to greet him. Bolan considered that odd. It was possible Jacoby had run into some resistance. Investigating the reason for the gunfire would have to wait.

He quickly sought cover behind the Bradley to think out his next move. If all had gone as planned, Jacoby and his team were supposed to be long gone. Somebody had to have escaped. It probably wouldn't be long before a battalion of well-armed infantry and armor arrived from the main post.

He remembered that Jacoby said that the Quonset hut was used as a makeshift garage. The Executioner needed some answers, and he needed to find a way to contact Stony Man.

It was time to have a look at just exactly what was inside that hut.

CUTTING THROUGH the rear fences of Fort Carson proved easy for Nahum and the men who followed him in an eighteen-foot moving truck. The vehicle was full of Kahane soldiers, and they had penetrated Fort Carson undetected. The group now made its way to the training site with Nahum's Hummer in the lead.

As they neared the concertina fence, Nahum could barely see a thick column of dark smoke rising into the starry sky and hear the sound of Uzi fire.

Nahum ordered Mikael to increase speed while he leaned into the back seat of the Hummer and grabbed the handset of a field radio. He quickly set the dial to the prearranged frequency, then keyed the handset. When the leader of the penetration team following the Hummer answered, Nahum barked a series of orders.

"Our brothers may need our assistance," Nahum cautioned. "Be prepared for resistance!"

"Understood and out," came a static-filled reply.

Two guards at the front gate stiffened at Nahum's approach. The Kahane Chai leader didn't wait for an explanation. He jumped from the Hummer and stared hard at them. The soldiers stood in shock, the whites of their eyes visible in the lights from the Hummer. Nahum's face took on a dangerous hue of red.

"What is the meaning of this?" he demanded. "Answer me!"

"W-we were surprised by—" one of the Kahane terrorists stammered.

His partner jumped in. "We were almost overtaken by a few of their people, sir. One is a tall, dark-haired man we have not been able to identify. The other was the intelligence captain and his aide. The captain is dead, but we managed to capture the woman as you ordered. The American colonel is dead, as well."

"Did you have any trouble getting in last night?"

"We got inside the houses of the mock village without a problem."

"Sir, one of the American officers has escaped," the first soldier reported.

"What officer?" Nahum asked. "You just said that the captain and the colonel were both dead."

"We do not know where he came from, sir," the man finally managed. "We observed him arriving this afternoon."

"What is all that damned shooting?"

"We are executing the last of the SF commandos who tried to escape."

"Is our contact with them?"

"Yes, sir," the second soldier confirmed.

"Maintain your guard."

Nahum jumped back into the Hummer without waiting for a reply and ordered Mikael to continue. The shooting had stopped by the time they arrived at the site of the mock village. The area looked deserted. Nearby, Nahum saw smoke pouring from a Bradley. The left track had been dislodged, and half a dozen bodies surrounded it.

Nahum would deal with that problem in good time, but other matters needed his immediate attention. He dismounted the Hummer and ordered Mikael to wait.

The terrorist entered the village courtyard and noticed the SF commandos were spread out in a row, facedown. A group from the first Kahane team was standing around the bodies. Only one of the American soldiers remained alive. Lieutenant Ford rushed to Nahum, embracing his fellow countryman and kissing him on both cheeks.

Nahum studied Ford with concern. "Are you okay?"

"Yes, Nahum. The last of the Special Forces group has been neutralized. We have captured the Mossad woman. We are ready to begin the second phase of the operation."

"Good."

Nahum looked around and noticed that a few more of their men lay dead. A moment of grief struck his heart. Nahum knew such sacrifices were sometimes necessary, but he would never become used to the idea. He recognized some of the men—they had been dedicated soldiers and friends. Their sacrifices would be remembered one day, and the children of a new Hebrew nation would echo their names.

"The ACTEN device has apparently done its work on this post," Nahum told Ford. "They are in a state of complete chaos."

"All is proceeding as planned," Ford replied. He followed

Nahum as the Kahane lieutenant began to inspect the American bodies. "We have accounted for everyone except the American colonel."

"The men at the gate indicated there was another officer."

"Yes, a man named Colonel Pollock. He proved quite troublesome. He tried to use that armored track vehicle to destroy us, but one of our men managed to disable it. Unfortunately, he escaped and managed to slip out during the battle."

"The team I brought with me will search the area," Nahum said. He eyed Ford with serious disappointment. "You should not have allowed this to become so out of control, Ford."

"I understand, sir."

Nahum let it rest with that. There was no point in dwelling on the mistake. Ford was a good soldier, and Nahum was actually impressed with the control he'd exerted in the face of an unpredictable turn of events. He had done exactly as Nahum would have under the circumstances, and he wouldn't compound the error by overreacting in front of his men. Such behavior would only serve to weaken the alliances it had taken so long for Nahum to form.

"Where is this Mossad woman?"

"She is under guard in the officers' hut."

"Fine. Take this detail and get over to the area where the trucks are stored," Nahum continued.

"As you wish, sir," Ford replied.

"Now, I will go have a talk with the Mossad woman."

ILIA YASSO STARED at Nahum with pure contempt.

The Kahane leader's distaste for Yasso was obvious in the way his dark eyes studied her. Yasso couldn't have cared less. She didn't want to believe that her own people could be responsible for the brutal murder of a couple dozen unarmed American soldiers. The cold brutality of the war against terrorism had taken on a new light for Yasso. She struggled at the bonds holding her to the chair, but to no avail. Nahum watched her struggles with feigned amusement.

The Mossad agent spit at Nahum's feet. "You are a butcher. How can you call yourself an Israeli?"

"I call myself a patriot," Nahum replied angrily. "That would be the opposite of you, whom I would call a traitor."

"You murder Americans, kill Palestinian children and steal from your own government," Yasso snapped. "Yet you call *me* a traitor."

"There are two sides to every war, woman," Nahum said more quietly. "There is the side of the politicians and those who would sell our birthright out from under our noses. Then there are those who fight for freedom and do battle against our would-be oppressors."

"You are neither, Nahum," Yasso interjected. The Kahane terrorist looked surprised. "Oh, of course I know who you are. Mossad makes certain we are well informed on anyone wanted for terrorist acts against the government."

"We have never committed acts of terror!" Nahum exclaimed. He began to pace around the large, open room of the officers' hut. "We have committed only acts of war against our most hated enemies! The Islamic jihad has poured destruction upon our heads, and the despicable acts they perpetrate have gone unchecked by your beloved Mossad."

"Save me your speeches," Yasso hissed, continuing to strain against the heavy rope binds. "You and your men are pathetic."

Nahum stopped his pacing to fix Yasso with a cold smile. "Maybe you will not feel that way when Jurre Mendel arrives. I do not think you will be so brave when you see what he has in store for you."

A cold chill ran down Yasso's spine.

Mendel was one of the most feared men in the Kach-Kahane Chai organization. He was a hardened soldier of numerous wars and a renegade of the Israel Defense Forces. Formerly an Israeli commando, Mendel had joined the Kahane Chai movement in response to the loss of his parents. His father had been a highly decorated soldier. Mendel was wanted for at least thirty separate crimes or acts of terrorism, and he was a formidable opponent.

It was no wonder that the Kahane leadership would choose him for such a bold and difficult mission.

"I have my orders to keep you alive," Nahum stated. "Until we depart, you will remain here. Once I have delivered you to Mendel, you will no longer be a problem. Until such time, you will be treated in accordance with your behavior. If you test me by trying to escape, I will shoot you on sight. Understood?"

Yasso sneered at Nahum but remained silent.

"I will take that as a yes," Nahum replied.

With that, he turned on his heel and left the hut.

6

Mack Bolan crouched near the front door of the hut.

He swept the dark, dusty interior with the Uzi, but only an eerie silence greeted him.

Three five-ton trucks were parked bumper to tailgate inside the long building. The entire rear wall of the hut was covered with a louvered steel door that rolled up to allow overhead clearance of the vehicles. It was just as Jacoby had told Bolan—nothing more than a makeshift garage.

The Executioner checked the cab of the first truck and found it was empty. A subsequent search of the remaining two resulted in the same. There were no radios—contacting sources outside the compound was no longer a viable option. Bolan decided to check the back of the trucks. He flipped on his flashlight and spotted a tool bench against one well. Quickly locating a crowbar, he then stepped onto the bumper of the second truck to access the back of the first. There were benches along the sides of the bed, and two small crates inside the truck.

The soldier wedged the crowbar into one of the crates and pried. It wouldn't budge. He attempted a second entry along the side, pulling back on the crowbar with all his strength, but the crate wouldn't split open.

Bolan knelt and studied the crate carefully. There were no markings, and he began to wonder if these were the chip containers. He sorted through mental files, his photographic memory recalling the information Stony Man and provided about the chips. He remembered one paragraph of information provided by Kurtzman.

Immediately under the exterior wood of the crate was a self-sealing container made of lead and a thin sheet of titanium. This would serve to shield the crate from X rays, as well as provide structural integrity. Each chip was wrapped and individually stored in a box made of Kevlar, polybenzimidazole fibers and phenolic resins. This combination of polymer chemicals was the same as the compounds used in firefighter helmets. They were completely waterproof, capable of withstanding temperatures up to one thousand degrees Fahrenheit, and generally impervious to small-weapons fire.

There was little chance the chips could be damaged by anything less than an armor-piercing missile.

Bolan moved onto the second truck in the same fashion, but this one was empty with the exception of more benches.

He continued onto the third truck, pulling back a canvas tarp to discover three large crates, each stamped with Property of U.S. Government, Army. Bolan popped one of the lids and wasn't surprised to find M-16 A-1 rifles with M-203 grenade launchers attached to them. The other crates contained five thousand rounds of 5.56 mm ball ammunition and cases of 40 mm high-explosive grenades.

Jacoby appeared to have been ready to fight a small war if necessary.

Bolan traded his Uzi for one of the familiar rifles and rapidly loaded the pockets of his fatigues with spare magazines and grenades. That task completed, he secured the lids to the crates.

Bolan was stepping over the tailgate when he heard the sounds of footfalls and men's voices approaching the Quonset. Whoever the new arrivals were, they weren't speaking English.

Bolan reversed direction, shutting off his flashlight as he retreated into the shadows of the truck. The rear door was rolled up as he wrestled the tarp into position and wedged himself behind the crates and the rear of the five-ton bed. Bolan pulled the tarp over himself, cradling the M-16 between his knees.

He reached up to his webbing and withdrew his Colt Combat knife. The high-carbon steel blade rasped from the quick-release polyamide sheath. Made in Germany, it was versatile with a universal saw, prying tool, adjustable wire cutter and a sapphire sharpening device that doubled as a wire stripper.

The warrior wiped away the sweat that began to run down his face and choked back a cough. The odor of warm canvas coupled with the thick dust was enough to make him gag.

Bolan's mission had done a 180-degree turn. He would have to destroy the chips if it meant preventing the Kahane terrorists from accomplishing their mission. They would kill anyone who got in their way, and he had already seen too many deaths at the hands of these people.

The warrior couldn't risk an armed confrontation there. If they were planning on leaving Fort Carson, a better opportunity would present itself. It was entirely plausible the Kahane had taken out Jacoby and the rest of his team, and possibly they even had hostages as a last-ditch bargaining chip.

Bolan listened carefully, ready for the terrorists if they happened to check the back of the trucks and discovered him there. If it were only one or two men, he might be able to take them quietly. He heard the terrorists as they entered the hut, followed by the slamming of the truck doors.

As the five-ton engines rumbled to life, Bolan relaxed.

For the moment, he had some time to form an alternative plan. The thing he couldn't understand was how the Kahane Chai troops had managed to penetrate Fort Carson in the first place. If one of Jacoby's people did manage to escape, the Kahane wouldn't get off the post. The Army would seal the installation tighter than a drum, and there weren't enough terrorists to take on the entire Third Brigade Combat Team.

There had to be more to the plan, something Bolan hadn't figured out or been privy to. Either way, it didn't matter. The

Executioner wasn't going to let them succeed. He would stay in the truck and bide his time until an opportunity presented itself. Patience was his greatest ally at the moment, at least until he could figure out what the Kahane Chai was up to.

But when the time came, he would be ready.

THE EXECUTIONER CHECKED his watch and noted it was almost 1900 hours.

Dust and dirt was caked on his hands, leftovers from the dried sweat where he'd rubbed his face, and his body was soaked under the cotton twill of the fatigues. Bolan licked his cracked lips and swallowed hard in a parched throat. His tongue felt thick and coarse—he would dehydrate sitting in this sauna unless he found an alternative.

The terrorists had moved the trucks up to the compound. Bolan could make out snatches of conversation, but none of the Kahane were speaking English, and the soldier's command of Hebrew was less than adequate. Bolan fought back the urge to move, scratch or shift his position. His legs were falling asleep from sitting pinned against the warm metal of the truck bed for more than an hour.

The sudden sounds of boots striking the ground and shouting voices signaled their departure. Bolan heard the unmistakable thuds and felt the vibrations on his back as an unknown number of terrorists hopped into the back of his truck.

Within a minute, the trucks were rolling and bouncing along the rugged terrain. Several minutes elapsed and the vehicle slowed its pace, nearly coming to a stop. There was another short delay, then the truck lurched into gear again. The rough ride dissipated considerably, and the engine whined in protest as the five-ton vehicle increased speed.

Bolan realized they were on a paved road. A highway? If he had to venture a guess, he surmised it was the one that bordered the rear of Fort Carson. The Kahane terrorists wouldn't have been so stupid as to try an exit out of one of the gates. It would have looked too suspicious. That thought

led him back to his original question. How had the Kahane
entered and left the post without the Army being alerted?

There was another question for which the Executioner had
no answer. It didn't seem feasible the Kahane would try to
take the chips out right under the noses of the crew at Peterson
AFB. There would have been too many questions, especially
about the absence of Jacoby. Then again, the mission was
covert and there wouldn't be too many players involved.

Still, the Kahane Chai probably wouldn't have risked it.

Wherever they were headed had to be out of the way. Perhaps somewhere in the mountains? Possibly, although it
wouldn't be far from Carson.

Bolan decided it was time to make his move. He eased back
the tarp and quietly pulled himself away from concealment.
He lifted his head just above the top of the crate and scanned
the truck.

Two Kahane hardmen sat on the side benches near the tailgate, one on either side and facing each other. This wouldn't
be easy, but Bolan had the advantage of surprise. The two
terrorists seemed occupied, smoking cigarettes and talking.
They didn't notice Bolan as he emerged from the shadows of
the truck.

He crept down the aisle, holding his combat knife close.

When he was within a few feet, Bolan stood erect and put
both hands on the overhead frame, pulling himself upward. He
slammed his boots into one of the terrorists. The force nearly
knocked the man over the tailgate and out of the truck.

The Executioner dropped to the floor, fisted his knife and
lunged at the other Kahane killer. The blade pierced the man's
heart, his eyes glazing over before he realized he was dead.
Bolan had the Beretta out before the first terrorist could come
to his feet.

"Where are we going?" Bolan asked.

"I say nothing!" the man spit. "The curse of God on you!"

Bolan scowled and drove his boot into the man's forehead.
The back of the terrorist's head rapped against the metal tail-

gate, the force of the blow crushing his skull. The man's eyes rolled upward and he died.

Wind and dust stung Bolan's eyes as he stood on the tailgate and peered over the top of the truck canvas. He studied the convoy intently. The soldier could discern a sharp curve approximately one hundred yards ahead, angling away from the fence line that bordered Fort Carson. The other two five-ton trucks were in front, and the majority of the Kahane terrorists were barely visible in the back of them.

A Hummer had the lead—probably the personal vehicle for the Kahane leader and his staff.

Bolan dropped back inside the truck bed, retrieved his knife and worked his way toward the front. He knelt on the crate he'd used to hide behind, quickly cut the canvas on three sides, folded the canvas down and pinned it to the top of the crate with his knee. He sheathed his combat knife, reached down behind the crate, slung his M-16/M-203 and waited.

The Executioner estimated he would have only thirty seconds to get the truck in his control. Timing was everything. He would have to take out the passenger first. Bolan risked a glance through his scuttle hole. As soon as the rest of the convoy disappeared from view around the corner, Bolan made his move.

He came through the hole and grabbed the top of the bed, swinging onto the running board and firmly planting his foot there. Bolan yanked open the door and grabbed the Kahane passenger by the collar. He pulled hard, throwing the terrorist from the seat and watching him hit the ground headfirst.

Bolan was inside the cab in seconds with the Beretta in his fist. He pointed the gaping barrel at the driver's head as the Kahane terrorist turned a surprised glance in his direction.

Bolan squeezed the trigger.

The 175-grain hollow point slug punched through the man's skull and exited the other side, taking blood, bone fragments and brain tissue with it. His head slammed against the window frame, leaving a gory smear on the door.

Bolan whipped open the door and used his body weight to force the smaller man out of the truck. The doll-like form bounced against the sideboard before hitting the ground. The back end of the truck swayed as the rear dual tires rolled over the body. The Executioner fought the steering wheel to get the truck under control.

The other vehicles came into view as Bolan rounded the blind curve. They drove for about five hundred feet before the road straightened. The Executioner unslung his M-16/M-203 and placed it on the seat next to him.

The soldier had a truck now, but he still didn't have a clue to where they were going. Any diversion on his part would be met with an immediate response—he couldn't risk taking an alternate course.

What he needed was a plan.

Bolan used the drive to formulate his next move. If the convoy stopped, he would have to go EVA and try to follow the group by other means. They would notice their people missing eventually. He would have to wait until the convoy had reached its destination before setting a plan in motion. If he managed to destroy the trucks, he would effectively eliminate the terror group's transportation. They would be stranded, and the Executioner could then pick them off one by one if necessary.

The convoy relentlessly continued onward.

NEARLY AN HOUR PASSED before they reached the city of Penrose, where Highway 115 intersected Highway 50. The sun was dipping beyond the looming mountains to the west, casting ominous shadows where it was broken by the irregular shapes of hilltops and ridges. A cloud bank had moved in, as well, and the sky began to flash. The thunder rolled across the sky and echoed against the buildings and houses along Highway 50.

The convoy stopped at the intersection, and Bolan slowed his vehicle quickly. He wanted to stay as far back as possible.

The Hummer turned west onto the highway, immediately followed by the first pair of trucks.

Bolan purposely delayed his stop by almost a minute to allow a couple of passenger vehicles to pass. He made the right-hand turn and watched as the last truck braked. It was slowing, giving him some time to catch up. Bolan shook his head. He wanted to keep the passenger cars between them, but the cars were moving faster than the trucks and passed the convoy easily.

He increased speed and moved up close to the convoy. Traffic got heavier as they entered the outskirts of Penrose. Most of the civilian populace on the road didn't seem to give the military trucks a second glance. Such vehicles were obviously not a new sight. Bolan knew the Army moved along many of the U.S. highways, driving to other installations that were used strictly for maneuvers.

The traffic continued to thicken.

Bolan slowed to keep a couple of vehicles between him and the truck ahead. He was able to keep far enough behind to avoid detection by the terrorists in the other trucks when the convoy was forced to stop at traffic lights.

Hairs stood up on the back of Bolan's neck. He didn't like this—it was too risky. The Kahane terrorists were going to get suspicious before long, and Bolan hadn't conjured any alternative plans to his liking. A shootout in downtown Penrose wasn't his first choice. Then again, the Kahane terrorists might not want to draw such attention to themselves. The military was not a law unto itself, as in police states. Federal authority didn't supersede the civilian police and state authorities, and a gun battle involving U.S. Army vehicles would definitely draw attention and distract the Kahane from its mission.

If the Kahane Chai terrorists had any idea something was cooking, they would wait until a better opportunity presented itself. Bolan forced himself to remain calm as the convoy pressed on. Soon they were out of Penrose and continuing toward the next town.

Bolan watched the signs as he drove. They were headed to Cañon City. Bolan was familiar enough with Colorado to know that Cañon City was home to some major tourist attractions. There were no airfields nearby, large or small, that Bolan could remember. The Executioner searched the cab quickly for a map, and finally managed to pull a photocopy of the area from under the seat.

He quickly perused the page while intermittently keeping his eye on the road. A red *X* was marked near Royal Gorge Park, one of the tourist traps Bolan had remembered reading about. The map showed a second place nearby called Buckskin Joe's, and the Arkansas River ran directly through the twin attractions. There was also a railway marked on the map.

Did the Kahane plan to rail-load the chips and ship them out of Colorado to another site? It was possible.

Bolan tossed the wrinkled map on the seat and began to assess the situation. Okay, first the SAC and a bipartisan group from Congress lift the embargo on exporting 64-bit technology. Suddenly, Baram Herzhaft appears with his new ACTEN device and says he has the solution to counteract cyberterrorism. Mossad jumps into the act and sends one of its agents to arrange for an escort to a secret rendezvous in Israel. Then the Kahane Chai comes on the scene, somehow manages to waltz into Fort Carson and snatch the technology.

It seemed like a bizarre set of circumstances. It would have been easier to just arrange theft of the chips in Israel. Bolan couldn't understand this angle. Why would the Kahane have come to the U.S. to conduct the operation? Why not let the chips fall right into its lap?

Bolan wondered if Herzhaft or Yasso had the answers to any of his questions. The whole mission had gone sour from the beginning. The Kahane was up to something else. There had to be more to the plan.

Somewhere ahead, Bolan surmised, he would find his answers.

7

Israel

Baram Herzhaft knew the time to leave was growing near. His sources had already told him about what transpired at Fort Carson. The entire installation had been shut down, and their commander was overwhelmed by the problems. Mendel's men would surely be able to accomplish the mission without interference. Herzhaft didn't worry about the Kahane Chai. They were well trained and equipped, and they employed methods that got results.

Herzhaft was more concerned about Ilia. Without Esdras to keep him apprised of Ilia's status, Herzhaft had no idea where she was or if she was alive. God, she was important to him, more important than any woman had a right to be to a man.

He couldn't stifle his feelings of guilt. In a way, he had betrayed Ilia as much as his own country, and she might not be prepared to handle the news of Herzhaft's deception. She was a strong and dedicated woman—loyal to her country—but she was blinded to the larger picture by those same loyalties. Herzhaft thought, in time, that he could convince her of the necessity of his actions.

When Ilia had first entered the Mossad, Herzhaft was impressed with the bright and voluptuous trainee. She was quick on her feet, and every task assigned to her came with ease. Her natural charm was like an aphrodisiac to Herzhaft. He'd wondered if her seeming advances were nothing more than an attempt to increase her ratings. As time went by, Herzhaft came to realize there was something else to it. Ilia was adept at anything she undertook. She never gave up and she excelled in classes.

Ilia's education in America had tainted some of her views when it came to her Jewish heritage. Nevertheless, Ilia displayed nobility without ego, strength without dominance, and pride without vanity. Yes, she was a very special woman.

Herzhaft intently watched the computer screen on his desk. The ACTEN device had performed without error for a second time in less than a week. The Kahane would make good use of the device. The Palestinians would get their due.

Herzhaft didn't consider himself either an evil man or a man of violence. The very idea repulsed him. He had carefully chosen his career in the Mossad. He'd been clear from the start. No field work of any kind. He was trained in the use of weapons and unarmed combat, as well as espionage techniques. Every Mossad agent had to undergo this training. However, that's where Herzhaft drew the line. He was an expert in computer technology, not an espionage field agent.

Herzhaft looked at the clock. It was time to go. He quickly prompted the computer to download all information on ACTEN to a CD-ROM, and then busied himself with his office. The night before, Herzhaft had destroyed all paper documents related to the ACTEN device. When the download was complete, he would erase any remaining memory files and take the disk with him.

He pulled an overnight bag from the bottom drawer of his empty filing cabinet. The bag contained two changes of clothes, some toiletries and a forged passport. A voucher for one million Eurodollars was secured inside the bag's zippered pouch—his settlement from the Kahane Chai. The funds had been wired through banks in Zurich, Berlin, Salzburg and finally deposited into the account of a small bank in Athens.

Herzhaft had never been to the Greek Isles, but his physical traits would pass inspection easily enough. He spoke the language fluently and knew the customs. It was another gift from the Mossad. Herzhaft didn't have much practical experience, but he knew he could get out of Israel undetected. With the delivery date of the chips so close, the last thing anybody was expecting, even the Mossad, was for him to disappear.

When the computer had finished the download, Herzhaft dropped the disk into his bag and began typing furiously at the keyboard. He finally finished his task, then sat back in the chair for a moment and smiled with satisfaction as the computer began deleting its own memory files. There could be no trace of information left. Mossad had many computer experts working for it, and someone might be able to duplicate Herzhaft's work.

He rose from his chair, grabbed his bag, killed the lights, then left his office for the last time. He'd reached the bank of elevators in the Mossad building when he noticed two men at the far end of the hallway. They were large, surly types and wore three-piece suits. The men walked toward him and as they drew closer, Herzhaft realized he didn't recognize either man. That floor of the building housed the cyberintel and internal-security divisions of the Mossad, which pretty much narrowed the list of personnel.

Herzhaft pretended not to be concerned, whistling softly to himself and watching the computer display next to the elevator doors. The number increased with regularity, then stopped suddenly. Someone was getting off or on three floors below. The two men were close now.

He could feel his heart thudding in his chest. His ears began to ring as a lump of fear formed in his throat. Surely, his superiors couldn't have suspected something. Not this soon anyway. Herzhaft had been very careful and taken all precautions in his dealings with the Kahane. It was possible he could have slipped up somewhere. In the tension of the moment, Herzhaft was hard pressed to figure out where he'd made a mistake.

The elevator doors finally opened just as the two men

reached him. Herzhaft quickly stepped into the lift and pressed the button that would take him to the ground level. The men rushed into the elevator at the last second. Herzhaft was panicked now. There was nowhere to go. He had unwittingly trapped himself!

The men nodded at Herzhaft, who returned the gesture with a nervous smile. They turned their backs to him and continued a conversation in which they had obviously been engaged prior to now. Neither man gave Herzhaft a second look. They walked off the elevator as soon as the doors opened and continued on their way.

Herzhaft was disgusted with himself. He was acting paranoid, and making it obvious. He knew he was going to have to relax when he reached the airport in Tel Aviv. Customs officers were trained to watch for people acting oddly. Herzhaft might have fooled the two agents from the elevator, but another slip up like that and he would be immediately detained and questioned at the airport.

"Dr. Herzhaft?" a voice called behind him as he was nearing the building exit.

Herzhaft whirled to see a young man from his division. The computer expert was still sweating profusely and somewhat jumpy from his imagined fear of the two men. He forced another smile as he pulled a handkerchief from the breast pocket of his coat and dabbed his forehead.

"Yes, Matthias, what is it?"

Matthias was a young, eager man of about twenty-six. He practically worshiped Herzhaft and the man's expertise on cyberterrorism. The older man had allowed Matthias to work with him now and again, and Mossad had found good use for the boy genius in other matters.

"There was a message for you, sir," Matthias stated, digging into his pocket and sheepishly handing Herzhaft a piece of paper. "I apologize for not giving this to you earlier, Doctor. The man said it was important. I really am sorry."

"That's quite all right, Matthias."

The young man blushed, then looked down and noticed the bag in Herzhaft's hand. He studied the older man's face with curiosity. "Are you going somewhere, Dr. Herzhaft?"

"What?" Herzhaft replied blankly.

Matthias nodded toward the bag.

"Oh, no," Herzhaft said with a laugh. "Just some personal items I have to take to my sister. Um, Matthias, I will be out for the rest of the day. My sister is ill. I do not want to alarm anyone, so if someone should ask you, just tell them you expect me back later."

"Certainly, sir," Matthias replied with a grin. His expression became concerned. "If you don't mind my saying so, Doctor, you look a bit queasy yourself. Are you not resting well?"

"Not these days, lad," Herzhaft said. "Now, you'd better get on with that project you're working on. I think you're close to a solution."

"Yes, sir," Matthias boomed enthusiastically, grabbing Herzhaft's hand and pumping it warmly. "Thank you, sir."

Herzhaft nodded and watched Matthias practically skip away.

He felt a sharp pain in his chest, and a slight dizziness came over him. This was the third time in a month. Herzhaft rubbed his chest, more self-consciously than in any attempt to relieve the pain there. He was too young for heart trouble. It wasn't really chest pain. More probably, his stomach was upset from his adrenaline pumping and he just needed to relax more.

Herzhaft opened the crumpled piece of paper Matthias had given him. He put on his reading glasses and read: "Meet me at the usual place in one hour, E."

He was stunned. Was the note from Esdras? But the man had said it was the last time they would meet, and Herzhaft had not found any reason to doubt that. There was something wrong here. He couldn't shake the horrible feeling. If the note *was* from Esdras, then something might have happened to Ilia. If not, Herzhaft could very well be walking into a trap. Maybe the Kahane Chai wanted to kill him. Perhaps even Mossad would be lying in wait.

It only took a moment for him to make his decision. He couldn't take the chance that it wasn't Esdras with important news about Ilia. He would have to go. Beside the fact, Esdras always met him at the small café. The ex-Mossad agent felt safe there for some strange reason. Who else could it have been?

Herzhaft crumpled the note, shoved it in the pocket of his trousers, then returned his glasses to his coat pocket. He spun on his heel and headed for the exit as he checked his watch. There was still time before he had to leave for Tel Aviv.

Yes, Greece would just have to wait.

HERZHAFT ENTERED the dark, smoky café where he'd met Esdras many times before. His eyes scanned the room in search of the ex-Mossad agent, but the man was nowhere to be found. Herzhaft wondered if he'd misunderstood. Perhaps Esdras was waiting for him in the back. Herzhaft clutched his bag tightly against his side as he passed through the standing crowd of drunken patrons.

The din of conversation buzzed in his head like a swarm of angry hornets. The chest pain had dissipated considerably, but Herzhaft still felt cold droplets of sweat on his face and neck. His stomach was twisted in knots, and he couldn't shake the nausea. As he neared the door that led into the private cubicle, a weird sense of foreboding swept over him and increased his discomfort.

Relax, he told himself. Just relax.

Herzhaft opened the door and stepped inside the back room. A single exposed bulb burned dimly over the six men waiting there. They were dressed in desert fatigues and toting Galil assault rifles. Herzhaft immediately noticed Esdras seated at a chair in the center of the group of Kahane Chai terrorists. His throat had been cut from ear to ear.

Herzhaft backpedaled, stepping from the room as his mind

screamed at him to run. He spun on rubbery legs and rushed for the front door, pushing his wiry frame past the pressing crowd of intoxicated Israelis. Herzhaft had obviously been set up, but none of the men in the crowd appeared to be trying to impede his hasty exit. Herzhaft knew his weakened state might prove to be his own worst enemy.

The Mossad computer expert hit the front door and ran into four men dressed in casual slacks and shirts. The men grabbed him and held him against the door frame. One of the men leaned close and spoke to Herzhaft quietly in Hebrew.

"Dr. Herzhaft, I am Uriah Kelfham. I am a special agent with internal security of the Mossad. The director wishes to speak—"

Herzhaft cut him off, uttering an unintelligible stream of expletives as he pointed at the café. The abrupt sounds of screaming men inside the small building were cut short by automatic-weapons fire. A hail of rounds struck the thin door, blowing it from its hinges and driving into the closely pack quartet of Mossad agents.

Two of the Mossad agents reacted immediately, diving for cover in opposite directions as they withdrew Jericho 940-R pistols from concealed ankle holsters. Kelfham pushed Herzhaft away, then fell under a fresh onslaught of rifle fire. A dozen 7.62 mm rounds slammed into the Mossad agent's body and spun him away. He landed on the narrow sidewalk face first.

The other agent who had been standing immediately behind him was still fighting with the door. The agent pushed the door to one side and reached for his own pistol. Herzhaft tripped over the door as he tried to escape. His chin skidded across the rough door frame and drew blood. A fresh wave of chest pain struck Herzhaft as he tried to regain his feet.

The agent who had tossed the door was reaching for the pistol strapped at his ankle when one of the Kahane terrorists appeared from the dark interior. He fired at point-blank range and nearly disemboweled the Mossad agent with a sustained burst. The agent's body tumbled back into the street. A passing car swerved to avoid the agent, grazing the man's backside as it slammed into an oncoming sedan.

Pandemonium erupted on the packed Israeli street. Women scooped up their children and began to run wildly in all directions. The crowd figured it was under a terrorist attack, which wasn't too far from the truth.

The two remaining agents fired at the first Kahane Chai terrorist simultaneously. The twin rounds struck him in the chest and knocked the gunman back inside the café.

Two more Kahane Chai hardmen appeared, stepping aside to avoid their fallen comrade, and exchanged fire with the Israeli intelligence agents. They kept themselves behind either side of the door frame, careful not to present themselves as full targets like their foolish brother had done.

One of the terrorists scored a hit on the agent on his side. The round shattered the agent's shoulder and tore out his back. His gun fell from numbed fingers. Herzhaft noticed the weapon, scooped it up and shoved it inside his shirt. He fought to breathe as he made it to his feet on the second try and walked quickly down the street.

Herzhaft never looked back, but the sudden rise of intensity in autofire told him the Mossad agents hadn't survived. He turned several corners, then stepped inside a narrow three-story building. He secured the door behind him, leaned against it and slid to the ground. Herzhaft wheezed, fighting for air and clutching his left arm. The pain was becoming worse. He knew if it didn't subside quickly, he would end up in a hospital.

He couldn't afford this.

Herzhaft struggled to slow his breathing and bit back the numbing in his arm. Damn the Kahane Chai! Damn Mossad! Damn Esdras! And damn Ilia for wanting this whole mess to begin with! No, he couldn't be mad at Ilia. Like him, she was doing what she thought was best for her country.

Herzhaft suddenly realized he was most angry with Jurre

Mendel. Surely Mendel had known about the assassination. The computer expert knew he should have taken more precautions. He never should have gone to that café. He should have kept to the original plan and driven straight to Tel Aviv. He could no longer risk taking his own vehicle. Somebody would spot him for sure. The Kahane Chai didn't give up. They couldn't afford to go back to their superiors and report failure. They would comb Israel until they found him.

Herzhaft began to laugh at himself.

Was he going mad?

He wondered if the pain and lack of oxygen was causing him to become delusional. There was nothing humorous about his situation. He had to get out of Israel, and he had to do it now.

The numbing in his arm stopped abruptly. Good. He was feeling much better. The dizziness began to wane and within moments, Herzhaft was able to stand. He unlocked the door and peered carefully into the streets. The sound of sirens wailed in the distance, and he could hear the nearby *whup-whup* of helicopter blades beating the air. The Jerusalem police and IDF were moving in quickly to deal with the Kahane hardforce.

In the aftermath and confusion, Herzhaft was able to slip out of Jerusalem undetected via taxi. When he arrived at the airport in Tel Aviv, he produced his forged passport. It identified him as Nethaneel Uzziel, and he was leaving Israel for an extended business trip. The Israeli officials gave him only a cursory glance before allowing him to continue through the airport.

Herzhaft was thankful his physical attributes weren't threatening. He was thin and unimposing, and his rather mousy features kept questions to a minimum. He could appear to be just what he claimed he was. Playing a convincing role was something he'd learned well in the Mossad. In some ways, Herzhaft considered it too bad he didn't enjoy fieldwork.

The flight to Athens was uneventful. As the plane taxied to

the terminal and the passengers began to disembark, Herzhaft found his thoughts focused on the days and weeks ahead. He wouldn't be able to contact Ilia immediately upon her return to Israel. He would have to be very cautious. Timing was everything, and Herzhaft refused to do anything that might alert the officials at Mossad of his whereabouts. Herzhaft suddenly considered that someone back in Jerusalem might have gotten a good look at him during the firefight. Someone from Mossad had sent the agents to escort him back to their headquarters.

Well, he couldn't worry about that now. Most of the passengers aboard the flight had slept. Herzhaft hadn't noticed anyone watching him, but he had sent the taxi driver on a bizarre route to insure he wasn't followed and dumped the pistol in a trash can near the airport.

Herzhaft knew everything would be okay.

Two large men in suits suddenly stepped in his way as Herzhaft was making his way down the concourse. The larger of the two put his arm around Herzhaft and steered him in the opposite direction. Herzhaft didn't resist the man. The look in his eyes told him it wouldn't be a good idea.

"Dr. Herzhaft, come with us, please," the man whispered.

"Who are you?" Herzhaft asked quietly.

"Agent Brad Mosier, Central Intelligence Agency," the man recited. "You are now in the protective custody of the United States government."

"What?" Herzhaft whined. "You can't do this. It's kidnapping!"

"Lower your voice, please, Doctor. Unless you would like to return to Jerusalem."

"Um, no, no, that won't be necessary," Herzhaft stammered.

The agent pulled Herzhaft closer to his body and replied with a smile, "Just consider yourself a guest of America, sir."

Colorado

Akram Damesh drove his car west, staying far enough back from the convoy to escape detection. Wherever his hated enemy was going, Damesh would be ready. His devotion to Hamas was unswerving, and he had never failed his superiors. He would complete his task and bring the Kahane Chai infidels to their knees.

Damesh's three companions rode with him in silence. Samir Ryad, a burly man from Iraq and the leader of the group, rode shotgun. Sahir and Zaki, brothers from the southern part of Egypt, took up the rear seat. The four men kept AK-47 assault rifles out of view.

Damesh was upset. Their first two agents had failed in the mission. Rajhid Abduljaleel had been arrested and detained by the American immigration police, and Nadim—Damesh's childhood friend—had disappeared without a trace after penetrating the mission site at Fort Carson. Before his disappearance, Nadim had managed to pass the torch to other informants inside Fort Carson who were sympathetic to the Hamas cause.

One observer had noticed the convoy and identified Yusef Nahum as its leader. From the convoy's last known direction, it hadn't been difficult for Damesh and his friends to pick up the trail in Penrose. Yusef Nahum was a bloodthirsty enemy of the Palestinians and a resister to the jihad movement. His involvement left no question in Damesh's mind that the Kahane Chai was behind the top secret operation to destroy Hamas.

In time, Damesh would make sure the Kahane Chai paid for its crimes against the Islamic people.

"Do not get too close, Akram," Ryad cautioned.

"I am sorry, Samir," Damesh replied, easing his foot off the accelerator. "But I do not want to lose these men. I am sure they are responsible for the disappearance of Nadim."

Ryad glanced sympathetically at his subordinate. "I can understand your anger, but I would not advise you to let it cloud your judgment. You have always been a good fighter for our cause. I do not want to see you fall under the guns of our enemies because you were careless."

Damesh only nodded, keeping his eye on the convoy ahead.

"Ryad," Zaki piped in, "do you have any idea where they are going?"

"I cannot be certain," he replied. "They have obtained whatever it is they came to this country to steal, and I would now think they should want to escape with it."

"I must be honest," Sahir interjected, "when I say I do not like this. These Kahane swine are ruthless savages, but they are not stupid. They are many and we are few. They will be prepared for any resistance."

"Not to mention," Damesh added, "that there are probably more soldiers at their base of operations. We could be outnumbered."

"I understand your concerns," Ryad mumbled, "but you must be patient. If there are too many of them, we will call for reinforcements. I do not intend to die today without reason. I will not lead you into any situation in which we do not have the advantage, my friends."

Ryad's words seemed to soothe the group, and the men fell silent again.

The convoy entered Cañon City and continued along Highway 50 until they reached an uphill curve. The lead vehicle made a sudden left turn, and the first two trucks followed.

Damesh noticed something strange about the rear truck. It paused at the turn, giving the other vehicles sufficient time to forge ahead. The truck was stopped in the left-turn lane, but there was no oncoming traffic.

A sign on the right shoulder pointed in the direction of the turn; Damesh couldn't read it.

"What is he waiting for?" Damesh asked impatiently.

"I do not know," Ryad answered. "It seems to me that this vehicle has been trailing the others since we first spotted them." His eyes narrowed. "Almost as if the driver is doing it on purpose."

"It is possible they have detected us?" Sahir asked.

"Perhaps."

The truck suddenly lurched into gear and made the turn, and Damesh had to stop to allow oncoming cars to pass before he could follow. The road wound through harrowing twists and turns, and the truck repeatedly disappeared around the sharp bends. Trees lined the roadway on both sides.

A steady rain began to hammer their rented sedan.

MACK BOLAN SPOTTED the sedan five minutes before the convoy turned onto the road that led to Royal Gorge Park. Common sense dictated the four men inside weren't tourists—it was late and the park was closed. Bolan couldn't make out the faces, even when they were illuminated by streetlights and the headlights of oncoming traffic.

The soldier's mind began to work on this new turn of events. Whoever the men were, they seemed intent on staying with the convoy. Bolan knew he couldn't risk a confrontation. There were too many bystanders present, and no room to fire or maneuver. If Bolan was going to deal with these new players to the game, he would have to abandon his wheels.

The Executioner put the truck in gear and made the left turn just as a small line of oncoming cars approached. He checked his mirror and saw the driver of the sedan wasn't willing to risk a collision. Bolan dropped the gearshift into second to increase torque and engine power. He wanted to put as much distance between his vehicle and the sedan as possible.

Bolan rounded a curve. He stopped the truck, killed the engine and locked the emergency brake before exiting. He scrambled up a hill to his left and entered a cover of dense foliage. The Executioner checked his Desert Eagle, holstered it, then popped an HE grenade into his stolen M-16/M-203. Bolan chose a spot on the high ground that would conceal him while still affording a perfect view of the truck.

He crouched in the rain and darkness and waited.

DAMESH ROUNDED a sharp turn and suddenly leaned on his brakes. The car slid to a halt within feet of the truck, which had stopped dead in the road. The Hamas terrorists sat inside the sedan, watching the truck intently through the intermittent movement of the windshield wipers and their high beams.

"Something is wrong," Damesh announced.

Ryad turned to the two men in the back seat. "Check it out. But be cautious."

Wordlessly, Sahir and Zaki exited the vehicle, keeping their AK-47s concealed under the long trench coats they wore. They converged on the truck cautiously, one man approaching the cab on either side. Sahir reached the driver's door and pressed himself against the wet metal of the cab. He called to Zaki, and the two men jumped onto the running boards simultaneously. Sahir's eyes widened with surprise.

The truck cab was empty.

YUSEF NAHUM'S Hummer entered the parking area of Royal Gorge Park and swung around before coming to a stop. He climbed from the front seat and stood expectantly with his hands on his hips as the first truck appeared around the sharp bend, then the second. As the five-ton trucks did U-turns in the parking lot, an odd expression distorted Nahum's features.

A minute ticked by before he turned to Ford, who was seated inside the back of the Hummer. Ford had a .45-caliber pistol trained on Yasso, who was seated next to him. The beautiful Mossad agent stared daggers at the men, but they simply ignored her.

"Something is wrong," Nahum declared.

Ford looked at the Kahane leader with surprise. "What do you mean?"

"I do not see our other truck."

"Maybe he was delayed at the turn," Ford speculated.

"I have learned to trust my instincts," Nahum replied, his voice taking on a dangerous undertone. He gestured toward Yasso. "Leave the Mossad bitch with me, and take Mikael back down that road. Find out what happened to the other truck."

Ford opened the door and roughly hauled Yasso from the truck, then climbed into the front seat and ordered Mikael to drive. Mikael put the Hummer in gear and roared away from the parking lot.

The two men rode along the winding road for nearly a half mile before rounding a corner and stopping suddenly. The missing truck was parked thirty meters ahead. Mikael and Ford noticed two men standing on the running boards of the cab. They were dressed in trench coats, and neither of the men were part of the Kahane Chai group.

"Look!" Mikael hollered. "I recognize those men! They are Hamas!"

"I do not see any of our troops," Ford added. He reached into the back seat and pulled a Galil from the floorboards.

"They have hijacked the truck!" Mikael sputtered, reaching under his legs to produce an Uzi.

"We will deal with them," Ford grated.

The two Kahane terrorists jumped from the Hummer. Ford moved toward a nearby boulder for cover, and Mikael took up a firing position behind the door. The two Hamas terrorists had immediately spotted the Hummer and noticed Ford and Mikael bringing their weapons to bear. They leaped from the running boards, reaching for their hidden AK-47s as the two Kahane terrorists sighted on their position.

Ford and Mikael opened fire.

MACK BOLAN SIGHTED his M-16 on the driver near the cab and prepared to fire when the Hummer appeared around the bend. He eased off the trigger and watched with interest as two of the Kahane terrorists burst from the back of their vehicle and opened fire on the men. Shots rang out, echoing along the foothills and surrounding canyons as the foursome exchanged fire.

Bolan's eyes flicked to the sedan. The two occupants in the front seat bailed and rushed to help their comrades. Blue-and-orange flames from the various weapons lit up the area. In the flashes, the Executioner recognized the face of one of the Kahane men.

It was Ford, the SF lieutenant in charge of Bravo Team!

Slugs chewed up earth, pavement and vehicles as either side tried to gain the advantage. For a group of well-trained terrorists, their aim was appalling. They probably weren't used to fighting in this kind of terrain or weather.

The Executioner was.

Bolan used the diversion to leave his position and angle around the hillside. With luck, he could come up on the Hummer's blind side and take out all the combatants before they had a chance to respond. Ford and his partner were outnumbered two to one, and if their enemies below were Palestinians, the Kahane pair would have its hands full.

The Executioner would have to neutralize the situation quickly.

He came down the leeward side of the ridge and hit the road running, bringing his M-203 into play as he rounded the corner and approached the rear of the Hummer in a crouch. He was blind to the action up front, but his first concern was to destroy the truck.

Bolan went prone behind a rear tire of the Hummer and

flipped his leaf sight into position. The over-and-under grenade launcher bucked against his shoulder as the grenade sailed through the air and entered the center window of the truck. The bomb was a new high-explosive addition to the Army's arsenal. It was Swiss manufactured, weighed only 465 grams, and it could deliver two thousand foot pounds of energy per square foot across a fifty-foot radius.

The grenade exploded on impact and ignited the interior of the truck's cab with an explosive ball of red-orange flame. Superheated fragments of metal and glass, propelled by nearly one quarter pound of plastique, ripped through the bodies of the two gunmen closest to the truck.

Smoke surged from the cab, and Bolan popped a second grenade into battery before the remaining terrorists could react, firing at a point just over the smoldering, burning truck. It landed against the front of the dump bed, blew a large chunk out of the metal and left a molten hole of slag metal.

The Executioner rose and tracked the muzzle of the M-16 on the Hummer's driver, who had now turned in his direction. The man aimed his Uzi at Bolan, but he was a moment too late. Blue-white light dissipated in the vents of the M-16's flash suppressor as a plethora of 5.56 mm ball ammunition found its mark. An ugly red pattern of dots peppered the Kahane gunner's trunk, tearing through his body and blowing chunks of flesh out his back.

Bolan moved to the passenger side of the Hummer. He drew a bead on Ford, who was crouched behind the boulder, oblivious to the Executioner's presence. The terrorist's eyes burned with hatred when he spotted him. The warrior loomed over his enemy like a statue of death.

"I should have known this was your doing," Ford said, sneering.

A slight pressure on the trigger sent a score of 5.56 mm lead hurtling toward the terrorist, lifting him off his feet and punching him to the ground in a heap.

Bolan turned his attention to the remaining two men from

the sedan. They advanced on his position, firing their AK-47s. The soldier dived behind the passenger door of the Hummer just in time to avoid a storm of 7.62 mm rounds. He withdrew another 40 mm HE grenade from his cargo pocket and slammed the bomb home. Bracing the weapon against his hip, he pulled the trigger and watched as the grenade performed a graceful arc and hit the truck at a point near where he had placed the last one.

Flames and secondary explosions resounded through the night. The five-ton vehicle erupted under the repeated punishment, and Bolan's last shot ignited the remaining ammo and grenades stored in the bed. Thousands of rounds sizzled into the air or burned across the roadway as tracers and full-metal-jacketed slugs united in a singular explosion. Bolan threw himself prone, pressing against the Hummer for additional cover.

It was like the Fourth of July as one explosion after another resounded, blowing metal, plastic, glass and rubber in every direction in a multi-hued rainbow of destruction. The force of the blast engulfed the other pair of gunman, incinerating them as the flames expanded twenty feet wide and sixty high.

When the last of the debris had rained to the ground, Bolan rose and quickly inspected the carnage. The heat from the blast had been intense enough to bubble the paint on the Hummer's hood and singe its canvas top. He could clearly see the damage in the light of the flames as they licked hungrily toward other exposures. The explosion had caused the headlights and windshield of the sedan to implode and melted the front tires.

Bolan skirted the front of the Hummer and climbed behind the wheel. He powered the vehicle into a J-turn and headed for Royal Gorge Park. It was time to deal with the rest of the Kahane Chai.

Once and for all.

The soldier drove up the road and entered the parking lot. The trucks were there, and the Executioner saw no movement on the perimeter. He noticed an entrance directly ahead. A cashier's box and information booth with a pedestrian turnstile separated two gates wide enough to allow vehicle access to the park.

He leaped from the Hummer and scanned the area, looking for threats. It was quiet—too quiet. The sound of a generator starting came from his left, and Bolan noticed a sign above the entrance to a walkway that read Royal Gorge Tramway.

He headed in that direction, his weapon charged and ready.

THE SOUNDS of a gun battle and the secondary explosions told Yusef Nahum that Ford and Mikael wouldn't return. He could see the shadows from the flames, cast by the bushes and shrubs along the ridge that bordered the highway leading to the park.

Nahum used a pair of chain manacles to bind Ilia Yasso to a bench inside the aerial tram cabin. The Royal Gorge Tramway ran a length of more than two thousand feet at a height of almost twelve hundred feet above the Arkansas River. The tram led to the south side of the park. A trail ran from the tram's southern tower along the cliff face of the gorge and terminated at Royal Gorge Bridge. From a vantage point midway across the tramway, Nahum could supervise the operation and conceal himself from their new, faceless enemy.

Whoever was responsible for the destruction nearby was likely coming for Yasso.

Nahum meant to use that to his advantage.

His men already had the chips unloaded and were transporting them to the bottom of the gorge using one of the American site's rides. An incline railway composed of several upright cars would get their equipment to the bottom quickly and efficiently. Regardless of who was pursuing his group, the operation would be a success. If nothing else, he would serve as a diversion while his men finished the operation. They would load the chips onto a special boat stashed near the bottom.

If God was with them, the chips would be in Mendel's hands at first light.

"You will never leave here alive," Yasso told him.

"Spare me the threats, woman," Nahum warned her, slapping her across the face, leaving a welt.

A thread of blood trickled from a corner of her mouth, and Yasso sprayed it at him with her next words. "Fuck you!"

"A vulgar term," Nahum replied smugly, "probably picked up during your education in this equally vulgar country."

Nahum left Yasso lashed to the tramway cabin and stepped out into the station area. He gestured for one of the Kahane guards, pulling the man into the north tower and showing him how to operate the tram.

"I will be in regular contact with you over this," Nahum said, pointing to a telephone that linked the operator with the cabin. "Just do as I tell you."

The guard nodded, and Nahum turned and walked back to the cabin. The guard watched nervously as a fresh set of explosions sounded closer. Nahum closed the door to the tram cabin, unaffected by the new turn of events. He needed to show confidence even in the face of danger. Otherwise, his men would neither respect him nor obey him. Obedience and loyalty were absolutely necessary in leadership.

Once he had secured them inside the tram, Nahum picked up the cabin phone and ordered the guard to proceed. The guard hesitated—the sounds of battle were very close now. The guard locked eyes with Nahum a moment before he threw a switch to power up the tram.

A sudden sound to his right diverted the guard's attention a split second after he started to ease the lever on the panel that would send the tram on its way. The Kahane terrorist's partner fell under a hail of automatic-weapons fire.

Nahum watched with shock as one of his men flopped to the ground and twitched in the throes of death. A tall, dark figure in camouflage fatigues and armed to the teeth appeared just behind the fallen guard, turning his weapon on the cable operator as the tram began to ease out of the station.

Seconds later, the windows of the north tower exploded and

Nahum's remaining guard disappeared in a maelstrom of M-16 slugs and flying shards of glass.

Nahum felt a stab of fear in his gut as the shadowy form never broke stride. Amazement and shock beset him when the ghostly wraith rushed the tram.

As the cabin cleared the station platform, the figure leaped out over the dark abyss.

9

Mack Bolan's heart pounded in his ears as he soared through the air.

A cool wind brushed his face and the soldier squinted, focusing his entire energy to a point where a metal bar encircled the tram cabin. He latched on to the bar with one hand, the other grasping the M-16/M-203. Bolan's body arced downward and slammed hard against the lower body of the cab.

He looked down for only a split second. There was nothing but blackness beyond his boots, broken by wisps of white from the rapids churned by the Arkansas river. The bottom of the cabin met him at the thighs. He fought to sling the M-16 combo onto his shoulder, then managed to get his other hand wrapped around the bar.

The stillness of the Rocky Mountain night was broken only by the rushing wind. A stiff breeze rocked the tram cabin as it continued to advance across the nearly half-mile gap. Bolan could feel the vibrations under his hands as the cabin swayed in the winds.

A sudden gust threatened to tear the soldier from his perch.

Bolan gritted his teeth and began to pull himself up. He could see Yasso's face as she lashed out and kicked her captor, and was only half-surprised to see her alive. It answered a few questions, but right now he had more important things on his mind. He didn't recognize the man Yasso was fighting, but at that point it didn't really matter.

Bolan clenched his teeth tighter as he pulled. He stretched

his long frame into a horizontal position, and managed to swing a leg onto the bar. Maintaining his grip with one hand, he reached over his head until he could find a handhold on the roof, thankful someone had the foresight to put one there. It was probably used for maintenance.

The Executioner hauled himself onto the roof and lay on his stomach, studying the thick steel cables above him. The cabin continued to rock and sway in the gusts. At some point during his climb, Bolan hadn't noticed that the tram stopped moving. He looked behind him and estimated they had only traveled about fifty yards from the station.

He regained his feet and approached a service hatch, struggling to maintain his balance on the rocking tram. Holes suddenly appeared in the hatch nanoseconds after pistol fire sounded from inside the cabin. Bolan danced away, unslinging his M-16 and pointing the weapon down at the roof, careful to avoid the corner where he'd seen Yasso.

The Executioner squeezed the trigger, peppering the roof with a stream of ball ammunition. He waited until the rifle was empty, then grabbed the hand guard and turned the muzzle toward himself. He stepped to the edge of the cabin and rammed the rifle stock into one of the windows along the side, then rushed back to the hatch.

Yanking back the service door, he dropped into the cabin. His diversion at the window had worked, and the nameless Kahane terrorist was facing away from him when he landed. The gunman held a Jericho pistol in his fist, and the Executioner launched himself into attack mode.

The Colt Combat knife rasped from its sheath as Bolan stepped inside the zone area that made the pistol impractical. The man tried to backpedal and bring the muzzle of the weapon into play, but Bolan slashed his wrist before he could get that far.

The man reached down for his own knife in a cross-draw sheath, but Bolan pinned his arm to his stomach. The soldier drove the point of his knife into the soft spot of the terrorist's throat. He spun the terrorist in the direction of the window and tossed his trunk through the frame. Bolan reached down, lifted his opponent's feet off the floor and helped him the rest of the way through the jagged opening.

The Kahane Chai terrorist leader plummeted soundlessly into the darkness below.

Bolan wiped his knife clean on his pants and sheathed it, turning to pin Yasso with a cool stare. She looked at him, the surprise evident in her face.

"You okay?"

"Yes, thank you," she replied. "I thought—"

"I was dead?" Bolan finished.

He strode over to her and studied the manacles secured to the bench that lined the cabin sides. Fortunately, they had a keyless operation design and Bolan was able to free her. He tossed the cuffs aside, then retrieved his rifle.

The wind whistled through the cabin, and the overhead cables creaked as it swayed gently.

"What happened to Jacoby?" he asked.

Yasso's eyes narrowed and tight lines formed at the corners of her mouth. "He is dead. They murdered him, along with the rest of the team."

Bolan felt a twinge of regret. He'd respected the SF colonel. The guy had gone honorably, resisting terrorists bent on destroying the innocent. The Executioner had seen many go down—there were more lives lost than he could count. Jacoby had died like a soldier, and Bolan wouldn't forget the man.

"He was a good man," Bolan said.

"Yes," Yasso murmured. She studied him intently. "What should we do?"

"I'm not sure," he replied. "The first thing we need to do is get off this thing. Any suggestions?"

"We cannot return?"

"No dice," he replied, shaking his head. "We've stopped dead. I'm guessing it's a fail-safe built into the tram in high winds."

Bolan slung the M-16, then gestured for Yasso to boost him up to the service hatch. He crawled through the narrow opening and knelt, studying the cables with an expert eye. They were smooth and well greased. The cabin had a maximum capacity of thirty-five people, which meant the tram was probably serviced on a daily basis.

Bolan leaned through the hatch and extended his arm.

"Come on," he said.

She reached up and he hauled her through the opening. He pointed to the cable and noted the distance back to the station.

"Are you afraid of heights?"

"No," she replied.

"Then follow me," Bolan said.

He shimmied up one of the four bars that angled inward and terminated at a large pulley wheel. The soldier reached up and grabbed the lower cable, grasped it with both hands, pulled himself parallel to it, then encircled it with his feet. He began to slide along the cable in the direction of the station.

He risked an occasional glance back at Yasso.

She was impressively brave, following his moves without hesitation. Obviously, Yasso was one of Mossad's better agents. Bolan watched her as she followed him hand over hand.

Within a few minutes, the pair reached the station.

The Executioner dropped onto the station platform, then assisted Yasso as she dangled precariously from the cable. They scrambled up to the tower.

Bolan commandeered Uzis from both dead terrorists, along with spare ammunition, and handed one of them to Yasso.

He tossed her a curt nod. "Don't lose it this time."

"Yes, sir," she replied with a smile.

THE STOLEN C-141 touched down on the makeshift airstrip and rolled to a point within ten yards of the creek bed. The pilot swung the aircraft around, and the cargo ramp fell away from the rear before the engines died with a whine. The landing lights winked out.

Jurre Mendel descended the boarding ramp before it was extended and let his eyes rove over the Kahane Chai encampment. Six guards stood at attention outside the ramp, their Galil rifles slung across their backs. Mendel planted his feet on the soft earth with relief. His trip to America had been long and grueling. He was exhausted, and his eyes burned with tired indifference as they settled upon the familiar, wide face of Elrad Davisch.

Davisch was the site commander left in charge in Yusef Nahum's absence. The hulking man was young and impetuous, but his loyalty to the Kach-Kahane Chai brotherhood was admirable. Despite his ambitious nature, Davisch was quiet with an authoritative presence.

Mendel returned Davisch's enthusiastic embrace, nearly collapsing under the beefy hand Davisch rested on his shoulder.

"It is good to see you again, Jurre," Davisch boomed. "It has been too long."

"Blessings to you from Ben-aryeh Pessach," Mendel replied tiredly. "It is also good to see you."

Davisch nodded toward the plane and ordered the guards to begin preparations for the arrival of the ACTEN chips. He gestured in the direction of the command tent in the distance. The few lights that illuminated the tarmac faded to blackness, leaving only the light that spilled from the plane's interior.

The two men marched toward the command tent, Mendel rubbing his thighs to work out some of the ache. The hoot of an owl perched somewhere along the wood line reached his ears. The only other sounds in the camp were the hum of two generators buried below ground level and covered with tarps. Mendel took care to watch his step, and Davisch guided him toward the tent by one arm.

"You do not look well, Jurre," Davisch stated. "Are you ill?"

"I am tired, my friend," Mendel replied. "A few hours of

rest will be necessary before I can supervise the remainder of the operation. But tell me how we are proceeding."

"As far as I am aware, we are on schedule."

The men reached the command tent and moved inside. Mendel found an open cot in the dim light of the tent and immediately sat down. He pulled off his boots, then withdrew a gold case from his pocket. Davisch waited quietly as Mendel pulled a Turkish cigarette from the case and lit it. He exhaled a cloud of smoke, then turned his attention to Davisch with a nod.

"Please continue."

"There has been an incident," Davisch said after a brief hesitation. He lowered his eyes and added, "We believe some of our men may not have survived."

"What happened?" Mendel asked flatly, taking another drag from the cigarette.

"We are not sure. We have monitored the police and military channels as instructed. There was some kind of resistance near the American tourist park, this Royal Gorge. Nahum did not check in at the appointed time. He may be—"

Davisch couldn't bring himself to finish the sentence.

"Dead?" Mendel cut in quietly.

"It is possible," Davisch said with a slow nod.

Mendel's face fell. "That would be unfortunate. Nahum is a good man. However, we know that such sacrifices are a part of our war against the Palestinians. I have lost many friends and allies in this fight. Every death will be accounted for one day, and those responsible *will* pay. You have my assurances on that, Elrad."

"I believe you."

"Good," Mendel said. "For the time being, we will assume Nahum is still alive and the operation is proceeding as planned, since we have no true evidence to the contrary." He looked at his watch. "His team is scheduled to begin the transport of the ACTEN technology within the next few hours?"

Davisch nodded.

"That will bring them into camp around dawn," Mendel continued. "There is nothing we can do before this time, so we must wait."

"With all respect, I would like to make a suggestion," Davisch said humbly.

"I am listening."

"I would like permission to take a small escort down the creek to where it meets the river. I would need no more than eight men. If we have lost some of our troops, as I suspect, the additional manpower would be useful."

Mendel sighed and considered the request. Based on what Davisch had told him, there was a good chance something was wrong. Mendel trusted Davisch's intuitions. If Nahum was dead, it was possible his command staff had met the same fate. Yehuda, Mikael and Ford might have passed into the arms of God, as well. This would leave the team without any real leadership. They might be lost, possibly even short-handed, which could seriously delay the operation.

On the other hand, there was no tangible proof the operation was compromised. Garbled messages and radio transmissions weren't nearly enough to prompt such action on his part. If they were on schedule, sending additional support would result in a change of procedures. Nahum might be insulted or incensed by such a tactic. Moreover, deviation from their operating procedures always carried additional risks and required additional countermeasures to balance the changes.

"Either decision presents another set of problems that need solutions," Mendel finally replied, looking hard at his subordinate. "However, I am willing to compromise. I will allow you four men, fully equipped and armed. You will take a radio, and you will have six hours to assess the situation and report back. If in that time you cannot obtain hard intelligence, you will return here."

"Thank you, sir," Davisch said with a grin and a bow. "I will not fail you."

"Remember, Elrad," Mendel warned sternly. "Six

hours…no more. We cannot afford to lose anyone else this day.''

BOLAN AND YASSO reached the Hummer without further incident.

For all practical purposes, the park was deserted. Bolan left Yasso at the Hummer while he checked the trucks. The Kahane Chai had stripped them bare. He sprinted back to the Hummer, then headed south along a paved roadway that ran slightly uphill. Different buildings and eateries lined either side of the roadway on the north side of the park.

Bolan continued until he reached the bridge itself.

Royal Gorge Bridge was the highest suspension bridge in the world and hung over one thousand feet above the Arkansas River. It was eighteen feet wide, spanned a gap of 1260 feet with the main span at 880 feet, and had four towers that were each 150 feet high. Two thousand one hundred strands of No. 9 galvanized steel comprised each cable that suspended the bridge, with a combined weight of three hundred tons. The bridge had one thousand tons of steel in its floor and was capable of supporting in excess of two million pounds. It was completed in 1929 after seven months of construction, at a cost of only $350,000.

Bolan stepped onto the mammoth construction and peered over the edge of the railing. Flickering campfires on the shores of the Arkansas River were barely discernible far below.

The Kahane Chai planned to move the chips out via the river. The only question that remained was where. They were probably waiting for their other men to return. It seemed risky moving the chips out at night—especially over the rough whitewater of the Arkansas—but the Kahane terror group had already proved there was a lot at stake. They would do whatever was necessary to complete their task.

So would the Executioner.

Bolan left the bridge and returned to find Yasso in the passenger seat of the Hummer.

He quickly inspected Yasso's swollen and bruised face. Dried blood was caked at a corner of her mouth and traced jagged lines down her chin. There were circles under her eyes, and the expression of death was evident in her features. Even in that condition, he still thought she was beautiful.

There was something different about Yasso, some kind of fierce determination that seemed to propel her through the worst circumstances.

She was probably not unlike him in that respect.

Many years of soldiering and combat had hardened Bolan's body and forged his mind into a weapon of its own. His mental faculties were like a steel trap, able to process information quickly and even more capable of delivering death when the need arose. Yet it also wrapped Bolan in emotional walls that no one could penetrate. Perhaps it was these similarities between them that made him feel a kinship. Yeah, they were soldiers on the same side fighting for the same reasons.

Yasso finally noticed Bolan staring at her.

"Why do you look at me so?" she asked.

"No reason," Bolan said quickly. He lowered his voice as he turned his attention back to the bridge. "You just remind me of someone."

That brought a smile to Yasso's face. "Another woman?"

"Yeah," he replied with a nod. "Do you have any idea what the Kahane is up to?"

Yasso nodded and pointed to the rear compartment of the Hummer.

"There is an ammunition box in back. It contains a map that might be able to help us."

He retrieved the olive-drab ammo can and opened it. There was a folded map inside, along with a notebook and a red grease pencil. Bolan opened the map and spread it across the floor of the rear compartment. He reached up to his webbing, clicked on the flashlight and studied the map carefully in the hazy light.

It was a coated, color topography of the entire area. Royal

Gorge Park was clearly marked with a large circle, and a dotted line traced a path along the Arkansas River. The river ran from the gorge to a point where it met Grey Creek. The line continued about half a mile along the creek until it reached another flattened area that had been marked with an *X*.

Bolan opened the notebook as Yasso sidled up next to him. He couldn't read the writing and handed the notebook to her.

"Do you recognize this language?"

Yasso nodded, furrowing her arched eyebrows in concentration. "Yes. It is very old...a form of Jewish Sanskrit. This is a list of instructions."

"Makes sense," Bolan replied, turning his attention back to the map.

Yasso's full lips moved slightly and her voice hummed quietly as she read the notes. She lowered the notebook and turned to study Bolan with her dark eyes. Her expression was grim, and Bolan knew immediately the news wasn't good. Yasso looked at the map and followed the dotted line with a slender figure.

"This is the Kahane Chai's route. If I am reading this correctly, they plan to load the chips onto a boat they have stowed on the gorge floor and carry it down the river to this point. From there, they will turn off and follow this creek until they have reached their base."

Bolan nodded with a grunt. "That means they do have something set up back in the mountains. Does it say where they plan to go from there?"

"No." Yasso tossed the notebook in the Hummer with finality. "It is standard procedure to provide only as much information to each group as they need to accomplish an operation."

"It'll be difficult for them to get those chips down river. It's dark and the Arkansas has some heavy whitewater."

"They will have set up several alternatives, Colonel," Yasso countered. "The Kach-Kahane have proved inventive and resourceful in the past. They do not give up easily, and they will employ every means at their disposal. Do not underestimate them."

"I never underestimate an enemy," Bolan replied, pocketing the map and notebook. "That's how I keep breathing."

"What do we do now?" Yasso asked.

"I'm going to stop them," he said simply.

"I will help."

The Executioner jabbed a finger at her and shook his head. "Don't count on it. From here, I go it alone."

"You cannot stop them by yourself," Yasso protested. "You have already proved that. If you have any chance of preventing them from taking the chips, you will need my help."

"Doesn't matter. When I take them out, the chips go up with them."

"No!" Yasso shouted, grabbing his arm. "You cannot destroy those chips. My people need them."

He detached his arm and pinned Yasso with a flat stare. "And many of *my* people are dead. I don't have time to argue about this. There's no way I'll let the Kahane take that stuff. If there are going to be any other casualties tonight, it will be on their side. You got that?"

"I understand what it means to lose allies," Yasso said quietly with a pained expression. "That does not change the fact my mission is to see to the safe delivery of those chips to Israel. I will accomplish my mission at any cost."

"Not on my watch," Bolan shot back. "You've got more guts than sense. I know one way. I've identified the enemy and I have enough intel now to act on that. Don't stand in my way."

"Don't shut me out," Yasso stated. "I have earned the right to be here."

Bolan sighed. She was right—she'd earned her stripes. She had been subjected to more in the past few hours than anyone had. Yasso had watched good men murdered before her eyes, and endured the pointless brutality of the Kahane firsthand. He didn't have the right to deprive her of a chance to reclaim her honor.

Honor and duty were two things the soldier understood well. They were the principles upon which his entire campaign was founded. The Executioner was transformed by those very ideals. He'd used them to justify his war against the Mafia, and converted them to suit his purposes against the terror mongers and criminals of the world. To deny Yasso those rights would have been damned hypocritical, and Bolan knew it.

"Okay, you're in," he said, "but we do it my way and on my terms. No arguments and no second-guessing. Deal?"

"Deal."

Bolan dug in the back of the Hummer and pulled out two oversize Army ALICE packs. He knelt and opened one of the rucksacks. The inside of the pack was lined with a waterproof bag that contained rappelling gear and a two-hundred-foot roll of dynamic kernmantle rope. Three outside pockets held a change of fatigues, wet suit, several cans of rations and a first-aid kit.

Bolan grunted with satisfaction, secured the waterproof sack, then lowered the top flap of the ALICE pack and cinched the straps. He handed one of the packs to Yasso, then donned the other one.

"Have you ever done any mountain climbing?" the Executioner asked her.

"I had an opportunity when I attended college in this country, but I never took it," Yasso replied with a frown. "I am sorry."

"You'll have to learn on the job, then," Bolan said. "Let's go."

The granite walls of Royal Gorge dropped hundreds of yards into the darkness.

It didn't take a professional rock climber to realize that such a descent was treacherous, particularly under the cover of darkness.

The Executioner saw few options. They didn't have enough rope to rappel directly from the bridge, and he knew an approach down the tracks of the incline railway was suicidal. When Nahum failed to return, the Kahane Chai terrorists would be alert for any opposition and probably double their sentries.

The other problem dealt with time, and they were quickly running short of that commodity. Bolan figured he would have to find an area where they could descend with the equipment on-hand. A thorough search of the park turned up nothing, but he located a trail near its outskirts and led Yasso along an edge of the gorge that moved to the southwest.

The hill line dropped and rose with harsh irregularity. Yasso had a tough time of it, struggling to keep up with Bolan's long and measured strides. The flatlands and salt plains of her country hadn't afforded her training in the physical realities of mountaineering, and the darkness provided an additional hindrance.

Hardened by scrambling the jungle mountains of Vietnam, coupled with years of pushing himself beyond the physical limits of most men, Bolan had become accustomed to such jaunts. He occasionally slowed his pace to allow Yasso to catch up to him. Ground coverings of sticks and mud, softened by the torrential downpour, squished beneath their feet.

Yasso slipped and fell several times. Bolan was impressed by her prowess and stamina, however, as she immediately regained her feet and pushed onward. He smiled at her. Yasso seemed determined not to let him show her up. She was a competitive woman and not easily discouraged.

The path began to wind to the west, but Bolan ventured off the trail and scrambled south into a thick wood line. Yasso stayed far enough behind the Executioner to keep from being struck by the branches he passed. He moved through the undergrowth with surprising stealth, while the Mossad agent marched along noisily. The woman obviously wasn't used to moving silently through dense forestry, and she seemed almost inept.

Nevertheless, Bolan couldn't fault her. Yasso might have been a good espionage or security agent for Israel, but she wasn't a soldier and thus she wasn't used to his way of doing things.

The woods opened onto a clearing. Bolan crouched and waited for Yasso to catch him. She was startled, letting out a small yelp of surprise, as he rose out of the darkness.

"We'll go down here," he announced, pointing at a breach in the cliff edge, then shedding his rucksack.

Yasso followed his example.

The canyon walls were rocky and jagged. Darkness enveloped the couple, threatening to swallow them up in its infinite embrace. Yasso peered with hesitation at the barely discernible outlines of boulders and sharp, treacherous turns. She cast a skeptical glance at Bolan.

"It's the only way," the soldier said. "You can stay here if you want to."

"No," she replied, "I will go where you go."

Her voice lacked conviction, but the Executioner couldn't worry about that now. Time was short, and they had nearly a quarter-mile drop to the floor of the gorge. Bolan ran the numbers through his head and knew he would contact the Kahane Chai on the downriver side. If the terrorists had their boat loaded and departed before he could reach them, it would be impossible to follow them along the shore on foot.

The soldier yanked a support piton and rope from the pack. Buried beneath them were a rappelling harness, a rubber mallet and carabiners. He slid into the harness and hooked up the carabiner and figure-eight assembly to its front. Once he'd tightened the carabiner, he grabbed two pitons and the mallet, then walked to where they would begin their descent.

Bolan quickly scanned the wood line before selecting a spot that would facilitate the best position for tying off the rope. He knelt and pounded the first piton into a point just ahead of a small boulder. The second piton he placed at the very edge of their descent, pointing out toward the gap.

Yasso watched with interest as he came back and shouldered the rope. The Executioner carried his load to the piton by the cliff face and drew out enough to accomplish his task. He placed the remainder of the bundle near the cliff, then inserted the working end through the piton loop. He carried the rope to the boulder, where he wrapped it once, then inserted it through the piton behind that.

Bolan carried the rope to the tree he'd marked and tied a clove hitch and cinched that with a double figure-eight knot. He walked back to the edge, lifted the rope bundle and tossed it over the side of the cliff. He double-checked his work, nodded with satisfaction, then returned to Yasso's side.

He quickly assisted Yasso with the harness and hookups, then escorted her to the edge of the cliff. He picked up some slack in the rope, formed a bend, slid it through the carabiner and looped it over the tang hooks at its terminal point.

"According to the map," he said, "this drop is about 150 feet. We'll have to negotiate most of the remainder by hand and rappel the last bit. If you want to back out, now is your chance."

Yasso studied the Executioner a moment in the darkness, her brown eyes as cold and hard as steel. He could tell that the look said there was no way in hell he was keeping her out of this.

Bolan was acutely aware that Yasso had a score of her own to settle with the Kahane Chai. He also sensed there was something she wasn't telling him, but he couldn't put his finger on it.

It was a sense he'd learned to listen to. A sense that had kept him alive on more occasions than the soldier cared to count.

Yeah, he would keep his eyes open.

"Are you ready?"

"Yes."

Without another word, Yasso eased herself to the cliff edge and went over the side. Bolan watched her descend until she disappeared from view. He would know she was down when tension eased on the rope. His biggest concern was the rope itself. It was designed more for utility purposes than scaling walls and climbing, but it looked new, which probably meant it would hold their weight for this purpose.

If it didn't, they would plummet to their deaths.

Bolan pushed the morbid thought from his mind. As he waited to make his own descent, he considered the situation. His odds of stopping the Kahane Chai were narrow, but he'd faced worse odds than this. The whole mess stunk.

He had considered the simpler option of just finding a pay phone in the park and dropping a dime to Brognola, but what could Stony Man have done? It wouldn't have been practical. They couldn't just launch a fleet of attack helicopters and blow the Kahane Chai out of the Arkansas River. It would result in too much danger to civilians and a whole lot of explaining to the powers that be in Wonderland.

Besides, he only had a vague knowledge as to the area of operation. The map had no grid coordinates and no latitudinal or longitudinal reference. A search of that kind of countryside would take days, and there was no guarantee satellites would have been able to pick out the specific area to facilitate an air strike. Bolan could recall when an Air Force plane had disappeared in the Rocky Mountains and weeks passed before the downed plane was finally located.

That was fine. The Executioner knew the targets, and he knew how to stop them. If nothing else, he would gain enough hard intelligence to track the Kahane Chai to its base of operations and destroy it before the terrorists could escape with the ACTEN chips. For now, he wanted to shake them up. Without skilled leadership, they would make mistakes.

And Mack Bolan would be there to keep score.

ILIA YASSO FELT herself falling through midair a second before the hardened grip of her companion saved her.

She was tired, and that was causing her to make mistakes. She forced herself to remain calm even as he hauled her up to the narrow ledge—along which they had been inching—and waited until she had a foothold.

Yasso could barely see the bottom of the gorge. Flecks of whitewater danced in front of her eyes. The guardian angel in camouflage fatigues waited patiently while she caught her breath.

"All right?" he asked in a tight voice.

"Yes. I am exhausted is all." She smiled at him in the midnight gloom. "Thank you."

"Don't mention it."

They continued traversing the ledge in a sidestep motion, hands over their heads and constantly searching for handholds. Yasso estimated they still had another one hundred feet or so until they reached the bottom of the gorge.

The Mossad agent wasn't sure about Pollock's plan.

This kind of situation would have never occurred in her country. She had support and could call in artillery, air cover or any other such interventions on a whim. With a mere telephone call, she could solicit every available agent Mossad had to spare. There weren't uncomfortable questions and there were few limits.

Given her country's allegiance to its secret intelligence agency, Yasso had to wonder why Pollock didn't have the same resources. If he was working for the government, he had to hold some kind of special status. He wasn't CIA—definitely not the type. NSA was a possibility, or possibly the FBI, but he fought like a soldier.

Yes, Pollock was a warrior, but he was also a very dangerous man. He threw his entire being into everything he did. Yasso wasn't an idiot; she could see that much. It didn't matter to this man one way or another about the ACTEN device, Herzhaft or anything other than the interests of his own country. He was like her. He was doing what he thought was best for his people, and she was doing the same. For the time being, they could form an alliance based upon those goals, despite the fact they were on divergent paths.

Yasso couldn't get over how much Pollock reminded her of Tomas. She'd lost her lover early in life to just such a situation as she was facing now. Tomas had been killed when PLO terrorists firebombed his car. A subsequent investigation revealed the PLO mistook him for someone more important in the government. Tomas was a research analyst at the time. He'd been dead eight years now, and she still missed him terribly.

After his death, Yasso threw herself into a foreign-exchange program and struggled to learn everything she could. She wrapped herself in education, career, hobby—anything that would take her mind off her embittered past. She was finally accepted at UCLA, where she obtained her B.A. in sociology.

It was in the final semester of her senior year that Yasso met Baram Herzhaft. She was attending a computer conference for a special elective class in cybernetic communications where Herzhaft was a keynote speaker. He was immediately enamored with her, practically falling head over heels in love at the very sound of her voice or mention of her name. Yasso didn't mislead him, but she had entertained the notion of risking a new relationship. Her dates in college were rare, and despite the success in education, she was lonely.

Herzhaft finally convinced her to contact him when she returned to Israel. Another year would pass before the Mossad—at Herzhaft's request—would recruit Yasso. She proved to be a talented and competent agent.

Nonetheless, she was still a bit inexperienced. It took Yasso completely by surprise when the director of the counterinsurgence office selected her for the mission. Perhaps it had been the workings of Herzhaft, or even at his insistence, that Mossad allow her the chance. It was one of those missions that could make or break a Mossad agent's career.

Yasso meant to see it through, and Pollock was going to help her without even realizing he'd done it.

She hated to use him, but the chips *were* important. If it really came down to it, Yasso would destroy the ACTEN chips and let Pollock handle the terrorists. If Herzhaft didn't need the chips, then that would mean he'd deceived her in some way. Perhaps the Mossad suspected Herzhaft of some impropriety—something that Yasso didn't know. In her ignorance, she would have then been the perfect choice for the assignment.

She couldn't believe Herzhaft would have sent her like the sacrificial lamb to the altar, and there was no proof he'd done so. He was far more intelligent than anyone she'd ever known. His intelligence made him both strange and unusually attractive.

The idea was bizarre. He was practically old enough to be her father—he *was* old enough. There was a constant sexual tension between them; he cast romantic overtones at her that she couldn't ignore. She just couldn't bring herself to suspect him of wrongdoing. Had he betrayed Israel? Had he betrayed her?

She would find out.

The ledge suddenly widened to a flat outcrop shaped in a

half circle. Yasso stepped gingerly onto the precipice and tested it with her weight before trusting it would hold.

"We can rappel down here," Bolan said, interrupting her train of thought.

"Very well," she replied, pressing her back to the ledge wall to make room for him.

He stepped onto the ledge and shrugged off his rucksack. The closeness of him was almost electric. He was a handsome and rugged man, even covered in sweat and dirt, and smelling of gunpowder, explosives and blood. She gazed admiringly at his muscular biceps as he hammered in a piton near the ledge.

The pounding echoed into the night air, which had taken on a bitter chill, and she risked a look below to ensure no Kahane Chai arrived to challenge them. Not that she was worried. The big American could take care of himself and her, and probably not even break a sweat doing it. He was an impressive and attractive man, and Yasso couldn't help but wonder what might have unfolded between them in other circumstances. He was probably a tremendous lover.

The thought brought a smile to her lips, one he noticed when he rose and looked at her.

"What's so funny?" he growled.

"A humorous thought," she said coyly. "Nothing important."

"Get geared up," he said, pulling a harness from the pack and tossing it to her.

He had left the other rucksack at the top of the canyon wall, stuffing the remainder of the gear in the one he would carry throughout their journey.

As she climbed into the harness, her legs felt tired and weak. The ache of more than two hours of scrambling down the rock walls had left Yasso on the verge of total exhaustion. She was in good shape, but not like her companion. Something else seemed to drive him, something inside about which she dared not ask. She probably didn't want to know anyway.

Once she was in position, Bolan hooked her harness to the

rope and she slowly backed to the edge. As she leaned back at the corner of the precipice, one loose piece of rock and mud collapsed. Yasso lost her foothold, tumbled off the ledge and landed hard against the side of the cliff wall. Her left hand was pinned between the rope and the edge of the precipice, and her bare elbow scraped a jagged rock protruding from the cliff face.

Yasso let out a terrified scream.

Bolan reached down and held on to the back of her harness, then wedged his boot on the rope, sliding it away from the piton in her direction until he'd pulled enough slack to free her hand.

"Just relax," he said in a quiet, soothing voice. "You're all right. Put both feet on the wall and get spread apart. Find your bearing."

Yasso obeyed his instructions, curiously soothed by the patience in his voice. He was a good man and had saved her life a number of times, defended her interests, and now he was quickly but easily providing instruction to her.

"Get your arm behind you. That's your brake, remember?"

"Okay," she responded, easing her burned hand from under the rope. She took a new stance, planting both feet firmly against the ledge.

Once she was in the correct position, she smiled at him and he nodded.

"See you at the bottom."

As she dropped into the darkness again, watching his face fade away, Yasso couldn't help but feel a little dirty. He had helped her—selflessly dedicated himself to protect her—and she was still able to use him with a clear conscience. Well, if she was having second thoughts now while dropping into only God knew what, maybe she *was* exercising her conscience.

She descended slowly, easing herself down in stop-and-start patterns. Neither of them had been carrying gloves, and there hadn't been any in the backpacks. That was the least of their problems anyway. She could deal with that. What Yasso couldn't deal with was the nagging feeling she got as she continued to the bottom of the gorge.

Something was about to go terribly wrong.

11

As Mack Bolan descended on the rope, he realized Yasso was in trouble.

She was kneeling on the bank of the Arkansas River, dipping her hands in the cool water to soothe the rope burns. The two Kahane soldiers appeared from nowhere, stepping from the shadows of shrubs with their weapons pointed at her back. They were barely visible in the darkness, and Yasso probably couldn't hear them because of the loud rush of whitewater.

The terrorists hadn't bothered to wait to scope out their quarry, or to consider that Yasso wasn't the only person who might drop from the night sky.

Bolan hit the ground quietly and disengaged his carabiner as the hardmen reached Yasso.

If they were encountering Kahane Chai sentries, it meant they had come down closer to the terror group's position than he had originally predicted. This would make Bolan's job that much easier, and he wasn't about to blow the opportunity.

The warrior hit the two men before either could react. He moved in close behind the first terrorist, raised the Beretta and aimed it at the base of the man's head. He squeezed the trigger from nearly point-blank range, the report from the subsonic cartridge a bare pop as a 9 mm hollow point round severed the terrorist's spinal column.

The man was dead before he hit the ground.

The second terrorist whirled and swung his weapon in Bolan's direction.

Yasso turned to see the action and jumped to her feet. She stepped in and curled her fingers around the terrorist's hand that supported the Uzi under the forward grip. A look of surprise flashed across the gunner's face—the realization that enemies surrounded him on both sides.

The Mossad agent jerked the weapon away from him, breaking her opponent's grasp as the wide portion of the Uzi grip twisted. The man exposed his right side to the Executioner, who took advantage of the move.

The soldier stepped forward and fired a snap kick to the terrorist's side. Ribs cracked audibly under the force, and the hardman lost his grip on the Uzi. Now in possession of her enemy's weapon, Yasso drove the butt into the gunman's forehead as Bolan pulled his knife from his sheath. The job was finished quickly as he whipped the terrorist's head around, jerking hard on the neck while he shoved the point deep into the gunner's right kidney.

The terrorist slumped to the ground.

Yasso panted with the exertion while the Executioner walked to the shoreline and rinsed his knife clean. Once the knife was replaced, Bolan returned to Yasso's side and began stripping the two men of their clothing.

"What are you doing?" she asked.

"The only way we're going to get close," he replied, continuing to work, "is if we look like one of them."

"Won't they notice the blood?"

"In the dark?"

"You are correct," Yasso agreed.

"Give me a hand," he ordered her.

Yasso bent and began to assist him.

Once the Kahane Chai pair was undressed, the Executioner pulled a pair of wet suits from the pack. They weren't full diving suits, but instead consisted of a long-sleeved top and knee-length bottoms made from neoprene. There were also thin vests that went over the suits, which could be self-inflated to provide buoyancy in an emergency.

Bolan donned the suit before changing into the desert khakis worn by the larger of the two. The trousers were a little short, but the boots would hide that inconsistency. Once he was dressed, he dragged the bodies of the two terrorists into the underbrush, as much to hide the men as to provide his female counterpart with a little privacy.

Yasso had the worst time of it; the uniform practically dwarfed her lithe frame. The Executioner returned to find her dressed. He made some minor adjustments, then stepped back to study her.

"How do I look?" Yasso said.

"Like a midget wearing a tent," Bolan replied with a grin.

He turned and marched toward the wooded area from where the two terrorists had emerged, ignoring the mixed look of pain and amusement in Yasso's expression.

She set off after him.

The surrounding trees and shrubbery thickened and thinned with irregularity. Bolan moved quietly through the woods, but his companion tromped and thrashed, making an unbelievable racket in her progress. If the terrorists weren't expecting them, they would be now. As the first signs of the flashlights and the sounds of voices reached them, Bolan decided to stop.

"Stay here," he whispered. "I'm going to have a closer look."

"But—" she began.

"Remember," Bolan cut her off. "My way, my rules."

Yasso fell silent. Her downcast expression said it all, but Bolan couldn't worry about offending her sensibilities. It was neither the time nor the place to argue the point. He wasn't willing to risk allowing her closer until he had a good look at the site and could draft a plan of action.

He pressed forward through the dark undergrowth, keeping one eye closed, and eventually found cover behind a tree on the edge of the wood line. The operation appeared efficient and organized. Several men stood aside and directed the actions of the remainder of their group. Bolan did a quick count and figured the remaining complement exceeded twenty men.

Torches and flashlights on the perimeter of the operation illuminated two large boats that were tethered to the shore. The boats looked old. Their frames were constructed from wood and lightweight aluminum, and the shape reminded him of the old PT boats in World War II. They were supported by twin pontoons made from heavy-duty rubber, which extended from either side on thick rods. Two large fans were mounted to the rear and probably provided the primary source of propulsion.

Bolan scanned the site for the crates, but they were nowhere to be seen. The Kahane had probably loaded the necessary equipment—along with the chips—onto the boats.

He looked to his left and noticed the incline railway jutting from the cliff side. There were maybe half a dozen upright cars connected to one another. The terrorists had used it to transport themselves and their equipment to the bottom. There was no questioning Yasso's assessment. The enemy was both shrewd and effective, and the Executioner knew he had his work cut out for him.

Other than last-minute details, there appeared to be a minimum of activity. Most of the Kahane Chai group was seated on the riverbank or aboard the boat. They were waiting for their leader, probably pushing up the timetable to the last minute before they would leave him behind.

As if on cue, the group seated on the bank rose with a snappy order from one of men who had stood among the trio of apparent command staff.

It appeared they were preparing to depart with their prize, and this put a sudden decisive factor on the Executioner's probe. He glanced at his watch—it was midnight. One of the terrorists rose, turned and trotted directly for Bolan's position. He was probably ordered to retrieve the sentries.

There was no time to warn Yasso. At this stage, she would have to fend for herself.

As soon as the terrorist entered the wood line, Bolan got to his feet and took the guy. He charged low and rammed his shoulder into his opponent's knees. The blow lifted the man from his feet, and he landed flat on his back. The Executioner stood over the terrorist, yanked his head back and drove a knee into his throat.

Bolan regained his feet and unslung the M-16 as he stepped from the wood line. He raised the weapon to his shoulder, aimed for the lamps on the perimeter and loosed a short burst. Sparks flew from the lamps as their lenses shattered under the calculated fire.

Shouts of surprise rang out, and half the terrorists piled onto the first boat while their comrades spread out to provide covering fire.

The Executioner dropped and rolled as a shower of slugs from assorted Uzis and Galils chopped away the woods behind where he'd stood. Bolan spotted a quartet of muzzle-flashes in proximity to one another. He aimed the M-16 center mass, unleashing a sustained burst while he kept the stuttering weapon level.

Groans of agony were followed by the sounds of weapons hitting the ground. Some of the rounds from Bolan's M-16 chopped the torch in two and sent it flying into a container of kerosene. The can tipped over and spilled onto the group that had fallen under the warrior's deadly accuracy. The huddle of human flesh went up with a whoosh and ignited into a grisly funeral pyre.

Several more terrorists fanned out, ignoring the orders of one of their leaders who shouted while standing in plain view. The Executioner dropped the man with a short, controlled burst and sent him spinning onto a torch behind him.

Bolan rolled away from his position and got to his knees. He crawled back into the wood line for additional protection as the sound of an Uzi chattered to his right. He fired a quick glance in that direction and saw that Yasso had taken cover behind a tree and was picking out targets with impressive results.

The roar of boat engines suddenly demanded the soldier's attention.

He reached into the fatigue cargo pockets where he'd transferred the stash of grenades, popped one into the M-203 and set his leaf sight on the rear boat. The remainder of the Kahane Chai team that had been providing covering fire was boarding the craft in a panic.

Bolan triggered the M-203. The 40 mm grenade sailed across the clearing and landed dead center as the lead boat pulled away. An explosive ball of orange-and-red flames erupted, sending chunks of wood and melted aluminum high into the air.

The soldier had a second grenade in place and aimed toward the escaping boat, but it disappeared behind the tree line before he could make a clean shot. He began to rise from his cover when a fresh barrage of autofire changed his mind. Bullets ricocheted off the trees and bushes surrounding him, and some plowed into the ground immediately in front of him. Dirt flew into his face, and he brushed at it with irritation before turning his weapon on the new cluster of enemy.

The Executioner engaged the remaining Kahane Chai terrorists without mercy. He set his leaf sight at a low point just short of the far perimeter and squeezed the M-203's trigger. The grenade sailed from the gaping muzzle. The HE blast rocked the ground and engulfed several of the terrorists in a rolling cloud of intense heat. Flames spread across the clearing, charring vegetation as they burned a path through the wave of enemy soldiers.

Bolan slammed a new magazine into the M-16 and laid down a hail of suppressing fire. He could barely hear the reports from Yasso's Uzi as she continued to select targets wherever they presented themselves.

The Executioner fired several more bursts, loaded another grenade, then regained his feet. He broke cover and sprinted into a flanking position that put him directly across from the damaged boat. A few terrorists were fiercely engaged in trying to extinguish the fire that burned brightly from the center of it.

There was little resistance left on the shore. The surviving Kahane terrorists exposed themselves and attempted to draw a bead on Bolan. Yasso gunned them down as the Executioner aimed toward the aft section of the boat. He triggered the M-203, and the grenade struck the side, just above the water-line. A horrendous explosion rocked the entire area as secondary balls of flame and blue-white flashes soared skyward. A hundred-plus gallons of scorching diesel fuel washed over the area as the fumes ignited.

As the echoes of the explosions died down, Bolan dropped to his knee and swept the area with the M-16. The battle zone fell deathly quiet, broken only by the crackling flames of the decimated boat.

The soldier finally stood and walked into the clearing. Most of the flat, scorched terrain crunched under his feet as he marched through the destruction. Some of the bodies of the Kahane terrorists were burned beyond recognition, and a bitter stench clung in the dark air.

Bolan turned and looked at Yasso, who stepped from the wood line and trudged toward him. She stopped suddenly and turned her ear in the direction of the river.

The Executioner noticed her attitude of attention and focused his senses. As the ringing in his ears subsided, he heard it, too. It was the unmistakable sound of the escaping boat's motor as it slowly chugged away into the distance.

"They are gone," Yasso said softly. "We have failed."

"Maybe not," Bolan replied confidently.

The soldier had turned his attention to the glow of something just beyond the perimeter. It was faint competition against the flickering light from a nearby torch, and Bolan hadn't noticed it until now. He trotted to the object and bent to study it. The reflective material he saw was nothing more than an Army-issue chem light. The greenish haze illuminated a stenciling on the wooden crate.

A smile crossed his lips as he read the letters: 1 Ea. Raft, Rubber, Self-Inflating.

"Come here," he called over his shoulder.

The Executioner quickly opened the crate and nodded with satisfaction as Yasso drew up next to him. He reached inside the crate and yanked two heavy paddles from the top of the load. A water-resistant tarp of canvas covered the actual raft itself.

Bolan had seen many such rafts before. The combat raft was tough, reliable and easy to manage. This would help, since Yasso probably didn't have any previous experience on heavy whitewater. It wasn't exactly ideal for what the soldier had in mind, but he couldn't worry about that now.

"You are not serious," Yasso said. "How will we catch them?"

"We don't need to catch them," Bolan countered. "All we need to do is follow them. That motor is loud, which should make tracking them easy."

"We will never be able to hear over the river."

"Look, those boats are slow and awkward," he said tightly. "They were designed for hauling loads over distances, not for speed."

Without further hesitation, Bolan hauled the raft from the crate and set it on the ground. He quickly located the deployment cord and yanked on it. Yasso jumped clear as the raft obediently inflated.

"Go back and grab our pack," he told Yasso.

She dashed off without further protests.

The Executioner dragged the raft to the water's edge, then quickly took off his webbing and fatigues. He withdrew his Beretta and grenades from the cargo pockets of the trousers, then wrapped the M-16 inside the fatigue top. It wouldn't provide complete protection for the weapon, but it would at least keep the bolt and barrel clear of obstructions. He tossed the weapon into the boat and quickly policed the bodies for additional clips of 9 mm ammo.

Within a few minutes, Yasso returned with their gear.

Bolan took the grenades, Uzis and his fatigue shirt, and stuffed them into the waterproof sack. He then replaced the sack inside the ALICE pack.

He passed the Beretta to Yasso and ordered her to strip her outer clothes. Once he'd added their fatigues to the sack, he cut one end of a shoulder strap on the ALICE pack and lashed it to the raft. He cut off the second strap, tied one end to the Beretta through the trigger guard, then the other end around Yasso's neck.

"Let's go."

Bolan assisted Yasso into the boat and instructed her to take the front. The raft was large, designed to hold six to eight soldiers in full gear. The Executioner was the experienced rafter, so he would have to take a rearward position in order to steer.

Once Yasso was in place, Bolan shoved the raft off the slight embankment and jumped in as it rocketed away from the shore.

The whitewater was strong along many parts of the Arkansas River, and he knew with the onset of warm weather that the water level would be lower than normal in certain places. This increased the hazard from rocks and eddies, not to mention the danger of negotiating such obstacles in the dark.

The sound of rushing water rung in his ears as the soldier shouted to be heard above the roar.

"Okay, listen up!"

"I am listening!" Yasso replied.

Bolan could hear the tension in Yasso's voice. She was probably nervous as hell, and this would be anything but a new adventure for her. Whitewater rafting was an expert sport in many parts, and crashing down the mighty Arkansas River was bordering on insanity.

"Your job is to keep the nose straight! I steer and keep the rear end from yawing too far to the right or left!"

The raft suddenly kicked sharply to the right, and Yasso let out a startled expletive as she was nearly tossed from the boat. Her shoulders hunched as she tried to settle deeper into the pseudo-protection of the raft.

Bolan was taken by surprise, as well, but he clenched his teeth and remained calm, already feeling the strain in his muscles as he fought to correct for the sudden shift.

"Whatever you do, keep to the center of the river. If we run close to a ledge or line of rocks, find the widest and shallowest opening. Don't get too close to the shoreline, and watch for whirlpools. Do you understand?"

"I will do my best!" Yasso exclaimed.

"We'll have to do better than that, lady," the Executioner warned.

They were on a ride for their lives.

Literally.

12

Washington, D.C.

Hal Brognola sat in the safehouse and impatiently awaited the arrival of Baram Herzhaft.

Stony Man had many safehouses scattered throughout the U.S. that served a multitude of purposes. This particular one was part of a small condominium complex nestled in an uptown Washington neighborhood. It was a plainly furnished, two-bedroom unit that was crammed into a space of about nine hundred square feet. The condominium looked as if it hadn't seen use in a few months. It was dank and dusty, and the stale smell did nothing to improve Brognola's brooding outlook.

He considered his precarious position while he waited.

The developments of the past sixteen hours left no doubt in his mind that Striker was in trouble. Intelligence reports were spilling into the Farm every fifteen minutes. Major General Donald Wasserman had declared a post-wide emergency at Fort Carson, shut down operations and sealed the post. The Pentagon refused to comment prematurely. The defense secretary and other members of the Cabinet had advised the President to sit tight and not take rash action.

The results had left Brognola sitting on his thumbs.

Herzhaft was the missing link. The attempted assassination by Kahane Chai terrorists—an attempt Herzhaft had narrowly escaped—confirmed there was a link between the ACTEN device and Mossad's fears of Kahane Chai involvement. Brognola didn't need it spelled out for him. Herzhaft had obviously been working with the terrorists. Whether Herzhaft had sold the technology to the Kahane Chai for the money or some darker purpose no longer mattered. The man was a traitor to Israel, and Brognola considered Herzhaft's actions nothing less than espionage against the U.S.

Brognola was going to get some answers.

The Stony Man leader turned his face to the shadowy figure seated across from him.

Aaron Kurtzman's expression mimicked Brognola's grim resolve. The computer whiz hadn't said much during their early-morning vigil. His eyes were blank and tired. For the past three days, Kurtzman had worked feverishly to solve the myriad problems facing Fermilab. The Stony Man genius and his team managed to restore about thirty percent of Fermilab's systems. Kurtzman's team had remained in Illinois when Brognola requested Kurtzman hop the first plane back to Washington.

Brognola wanted Kurtzman to be present for the interrogation. The shutdown of Fermilab and Fort Carson wasn't mere coincidence. The 64-bit chips Fermilab had tested and those being exported to Israel were identical. Brognola was betting Baram Herzhaft and his ACTEN device were the common denominator, which meant Herzhaft knew how to fix the problem. With enough evidence, Brognola knew he could convince the President to allow Kurtzman inside Fort Carson and get the post back online.

"What is it, Bear?" Brognola probed.

"I just can't understand it," Kurtzman replied angrily, shaking his head. "I pored over Fermilab's technical documents, studied their hardware and software programs inside out and tried every trick I know. Right now, we barely have enough systems up to provide power. It's like trying to find a needle in a haystack, Hal. It's obviously some kind of new virus, but I can't determine the source."

"Don't beat yourself up over it," Brognola said. "I'm positive Herzhaft has the answers."

"I can't argue with that. Herzhaft's activities are definitely suspicious."

"Agreed," Brognola replied with a solemn nod. "After the shutdown at Fort Carson, I began to wonder if Fermilab's problems weren't simply a diversionary tactic."

"A diversion for what?"

"I don't know. Every time I try to come up with a reasonable explanation, I'm left with more questions than answers."

"It's a puzzle," Kurtzman agreed. "If these two incidents *are* related, the perpetrators have covered their tracks most effectively. Everything we've managed to discover at Fermilab leaves little doubt the problem originated from the outside."

"How so?"

Kurtzman leaned forward and rested his elbows on the table. Brognola could see a renewed energy in the computer ace. The paralysis in his legs had done nothing to affect Kurtzman's keen mind. A fiery genius burned beneath the big, gentle facade that all the Stony Man members had come to know and love. Nothing on Earth could spur that intensity more than picking Kurtzman's brain, and the man always managed to impart his wisdom on the less learned without making them feel inferior.

"Okay, let's say that you have a virus inside your computer. Theories of computer science say that the virus can only be activated indirectly. The components of the virus can't be downloaded unless the receiver gives the computer some action or direction, such as the opening of a file or the activation of a program."

"Let me get this straight," Brognola interjected. "What you're trying to say is that I can't transmit a virus from one hard drive to another. It has to come by way of a program or file attachment?"

"Correct. The Internet is a good example. Millions of people surf the Web and download information on a daily basis.

Security systems within browsers can be set up to view Web pages, but refuse to actually store the stuff on the computer. A few virus programs have been known to slip through in the form of cookies. These are bits of information that computers store about your identity, your computer system's layout, and your preferences for a specific site. This has a mirror effect, however. The tradeoff is that others can view what you're viewing.''

"My God," Brognola muttered. "Whatever happened to privacy?"

"There's no such things these days, Hal," Kurtzman replied. "Not when it comes to computers. This is where our problem with Fermilab comes in. Once we had their system up and partially running, I used my 128-bit decryption program to trace the source of the problem. We found fragments of codes, which told us the system failure was definitely the result of a hostile act.''

"Let me guess. You couldn't trace the origin?"

"Exactly," Kurtzman confirmed solemnly. "I'm telling you, Hal, whoever devised that virus was able to effect a direct shutdown. They penetrated the system undetected, crashed the hardware drive and split without a trace. The program Fermilab ran to monitor one of their fission tests simply activated the virus. Only small fragments of the virus were left behind in individual components. That effectively wiped out our ability to trace the source.''

"Will you be able to recover the system?"

"It's going to take a lot of time to clean out that kind of mainframe. Fermilab runs under a network, and that doesn't help matters. There are a good hundred separate drives working with one another, and the fragments are spread throughout the network. The odds are long that we'll ever be able to restore the computers to a workable state.''

"I take it this means that much of the information is lost?"

"Yes," Kurtzman said.

A sharp rap interrupted the pair.

Brognola rose and walked to the door. A whispered exchange of passwords between the big Fed and a male voice outside confirmed the waiting was over. Brognola opened the door and stepped aside to admit four men in suits. Herzhaft was sandwiched between the government agents, his expression similar to that of a trapped rat. One of the CIA men handed an overnight bag to Brognola and whispered in his ear.

"Welcome to the United States, Dr. Herzhaft," Brognola said, waving him to a chair. "Have a seat."

"I want to know who you are. What right have you to kidnap me like this?" Herzhaft demanded, his face flushed with anger.

"Sit down, Doctor," Brognola rumbled. "I am not in the mood for these games."

Herzhaft sized up Brognola, turned to look at the agents surrounding him, then opted to quietly take a seat. Brognola ushered the CIA men outside with orders to post themselves at the exits. Once they were gone, he took his chair, tossed the bag on the table and studied Herzhaft for a minute.

The Mossad computer expert was frightened, and Brognola planned to use that to his advantage.

"Let me begin by saying that my identity is unimportant, Doctor," Brognola said. "Moreover, you can be assured I have a direct voice with the President of the United States. The final dispensation for your crimes against both Israel and this country is directly commensurate with your cooperation."

"I do not understand," Herzhaft protested. "I have done nothing wrong. I have committed no crimes."

"No?" Brognola replied, raising his eyebrows. "I wonder if your superiors at the Mossad would agree, Doctor."

Herzhaft's snooty expression changed to a mix of horror and shock. Brognola was now certain Herzhaft had something to hide. The man's haughty belligerence had dissipated, leaving what Brognola deemed to be simply the shell of a man. He was in fear for his life, and Brognola could tell the initial resistance was waning.

"Your actions to date are suspicious at best, and you're walking a dangerous line," Brognola continued. "Why did members of the Kahane Chai try to eliminate you?"

"I do not know," Herzhaft said quickly. "Maybe they know I work for Mossad."

"There are many others who work for Mossad," Brognola countered, "and would present much easier targets. I think they were trying to silence you. I want to know why."

"I have no direct dealings with the Kach-Kahane Chai movement," Herzhaft spit.

"I never said you did."

A troubled silence fell over the room, and Herzhaft was becoming visibly frustrated.

Brognola had tricked the scientist into disclosing the truth, and the man knew it. The pressure was intense, and Brognola did not intend to back off now. A weight was obviously pressing on Herzhaft's shoulders. The Israeli wanted to burst, to spill his guts, and he was only waiting for the right opportunity.

Brognola decided to give it to him.

"Dr. Herzhaft, if you don't tell me the truth, I can't protect you. I'll have no choice but to release you to the authorities of my country. You'll be immediately charged with espionage against the United States, and extradited to Israel to answer further charges of treason. If I'm not mistaken, such a conviction would result in immediate execution unless you cooperate here and now. Even if your government is lenient and decides to imprison you, the Kahane Chai will get to you eventually."

Herzhaft's chin began to quiver, and tears formed in the corners of his eyes. The dim lights of the condominium couldn't hide the Mossad scientist's defeated expression. He looked like a man on the verge of a nervous breakdown. Brognola was relentless, repeatedly pushing Herzhaft to the decisive point.

"I am sorry," Herzhaft rambled. "I am so very sorry for

what I have done. I wanted to see my people survive. I am tired of the murder and the scorn and the violence." Tears fell freely down Herzhaft's cheeks as he continued. "Too many innocent people have died because of me. I have betrayed everyone. I have betrayed my own country and shamed myself."

"What did you do?" Kurtzman asked. "Was it the ACTEN device? Did you use it to crash the computer systems at Fermi National Accelerator Lab?"

Herzhaft would only nod in response.

"What about Fort Carson?" Brognola demanded. "Are you responsible for that, as well?"

"Yes," was Herzhaft's choked reply. "The incident at your Fermilab was only a test to see if the ACTEN device could really do what I had designed it to do."

"What do you mean?" Brognola asked.

Herzhaft wiped his eyes and visibly struggled to remain calm. "ACTEN is not simply a defensive machine, gentleman. It has offensive capabilities. It can shut down entire networks. It is capable of bypassing nearly any security system and destroying computer hardware from the inside. No other machine in the world is capable of such a feat."

"Then it's true?" Brognola interjected. "You really can send a virus from the ACTEN device directly into another computer's hard drive?"

"It is not a virus," Herzhaft explained, shaking his head. "It is simply a list of commands. Every computer with encryption or decryption capabilities operates under a set of security protocols."

Brognola looked at Kurtzman for an explanation.

"Protocols are usually standard guidelines or rules that enable computers to exchange information. They're designed to prevent unauthorized persons from seeing data that is sent from one computer to another."

"What does this have to do with the ACTEN device?" Brognola asked, turning his attention back to Herzhaft.

"ACTEN does not send viruses or false information into hard drives. This is considered a physical impossibility. What ACTEN does is rewrites the security protocols and subsequently scrambles the computer's memory. In essence, it turns the computer against the user and destroys itself from within. That is the parallel nature of its defensive abilities. When a cyberterrorist organization attempts to infiltrate a computer's security system, ACTEN sends a set of false codes and scrambles the interloper's system."

"Oh, my God," Kurtzman whispered. "That's why it looks like a virus. The rewritten security programs overwrite the current ones, and that's what results in the fragments. Then when anybody sees the fragments, they delete them from the system because they think they're eliminating pieces left by the virus."

"But what they are actually deleting is the computer's security program," Herzhaft finished. "This allows ACTEN to penetrate the device. ACTEN takes over and freezes the system until it is ordered to release it. While inside, the ACTEN user can alter, delete or insert data of any kind at will."

"Unbelievable," Brognola whispered in amazement.

It was worse than anyone could have imagined. The power of the ACTEN device went far beyond the amazing and bordered on the fantastic.

To a man like Harold Brognola, the practical applications of such a device were like something out of a science-fiction movie. Entire countries could be destroyed if their computers were penetrated by ACTEN. Cyberterrorism would be the least of problems. The ACTEN device could destroy the framework of everything from personal and commercial finances to political agendas. Millions of home computers hooked up to telephone lines or satellite telemetry were fair game, not to mention the threat against the global banking network.

The defense industries and military organizations of more than a hundred nations could be turned on their heads overnight. Weapons could fall into the hands of an unlimited number of terrorist or militant groups. Missiles, nuclear payloads and weapons of mass destruction could be diverted from intended targets or even launched from supposedly secure sites. Satellites and planes could be pulled from the sky, and public utilities across the world could be shut down with the push of a button.

The ACTEN device could also eliminate communication systems, tap any telephone line, pinpoint the signal of a single cellular phone or monitor dozens of transmissions simultaneously. Rockets and computer-controlled guidance systems could be thwarted or instructed to unleash a barrage of artillery on large residential populations across the world. ACTEN was a device of unspeakable power, and Brognola knew there was only one solution.

"Our agents state there was a CD found inside your bag," Brognola said.

"Yes," Herzhaft admitted.

"What is on it?"

"The only remaining source of information about ACTEN. All of my research is contained on that disk. I wiped the memory systems clean at my office in Jerusalem."

"Why did you shut down Fort Carson?" Kurtzman pressed.

Herzhaft fixed Kurtzman with a tired gaze. Circles had formed under the Mossad agent's eyes, and any sign of hope was gone. Herzhaft had obviously resigned himself to whatever fate awaited him.

"The Kahane Chai used the emergency to get inside the installation and steal the ACTEN chips."

"That doesn't make any sense," Brognola snapped. "If the ACTEN device can already do as you claim, why did you need the chips to begin with?"

"I didn't," Herzhaft explained. "The Kahane Chai needed them."

"Why?"

"They are planning to build another ACTEN. One they will use against the Arab nations. They are seeking retribution for the blood that has been spilled. Our people have suffered long enough. This is why I support them. This is why I have aided them in their cause."

"What would possess you to turn such a dangerous weapon over to the hands of fanatics, man?" Brognola thundered, half out of his chair and slamming his fist on the table.

"They will not succeed. There is a woman inside your military, escort...a Mossad agent named Ilia Yasso. She is my only reason for living, and she is my one guarantee."

"Guarantee for what?"

"There was an agreement between me and one of their leaders, Jurre Mendel. He promised to bring Ilia back alive. If she is not delivered safely to me, I will not provide the rest of the specifications. Mendel has a disk that has only part of the design parameters."

Brognola slowly sat down and stared daggers at Herzhaft.

"Do you have any idea," Brognola growled, his face turning a dangerous hue, "how many lives are at risk because of your little scheme, Doctor? Important lives. *Very* important lives."

"I am sorry," Herzhaft said. "I will assist you in setting things right. I can reverse the process and restore the systems I have damaged. Yes, I will help you."

"You're goddamned right you will," Brognola growled. "And you had better pray that our man inside Fort Carson is still alive."

13

Colorado

Large sprays of icy water doused Bolan and Yasso.

The Executioner kept an eye on his companion. Thus far, she was doing okay. He was feeling the chill of the water down to the bone, and his muscles ached. In comparison to his large frame, Yasso's body surface area made her the more likely candidate for hypothermia. She was accustomed to desert country, and her body wouldn't be used to lower temperatures. The last thing Bolan needed was for her to lose her faculties.

They were traveling at a considerable speed, and it was difficult to keep far enough back to prevent overtaking the boat ahead. Bolan figured about ten to twelve Kahane Chai terrorists had escaped in the craft. For all practical purposes, they were making good time. He estimated they would reach Grey Creek within the hour.

Yasso shouted for his attention and pointed directly ahead of them. The sheer sizes of the whitecaps he saw were dwarfed only by the sounds of raging water as they drew closer. Their raft began to increase speed, and Bolan knew they were in for the ride of a lifetime. The soldier leaned forward a moment and pointed to a spot near the left shore. The water didn't look nearly as rough there, and it was out far enough that they wouldn't run to ground.

Yasso nodded and began to turn the nose of the raft in that direction.

The Executioner settled back into the rear and drove his paddle hard into the water on the left side of the raft. Every muscle was taut with the strain, and he clenched his teeth to fight the fresh torrents of cold spray soaking his face. The raft began to yaw to the right, and Bolan switched the paddle to that side with the lightning reflexes that had saved his life more times than he could count.

The raft righted itself some, but the forces drawing them toward the center of the river were too strong. A new and unexpected current altered their course. The raft swung around and rushed its occupants backward toward the heavy whitecaps.

"Turn around!" Bolan yelled, reversing direction inside the raft and settling deep inside on his knees.

The soldier realized it was too late. There was no way they could avoid the obstacle course of sharp rocks and churning water in time now. He knew he would have to direct the nose of the raft around the rocks. It would be no mean feat in the dark. As the first loomed suddenly upon them, he dipped his paddle into the left side and pushed the nose away just in time to avoid the sharp rock.

Yasso wasn't as lucky. The rear portion slammed against the rock and rebounded with unbelievable force. The jolt nearly knocked both of them from the raft. The rear end yawed the opposite way, but never made a complete turn due to a second, large boulder protruding from the rushing waters. The right side hit this time, although it wasn't with nearly as much force.

Bolan was angry, but there was nothing he could do about it. Yasso was doing her best. He couldn't fault the spunky Mossad agent for that. He called to her but didn't take his eyes from the river ahead.

"Put your paddle into the opposite direction you want the rear to go! Control the turns switching to the opposite side!"

"I am *trying!*" she replied vehemently. "Look out!"

Bolan saw the dropoff at the same moment. It stretched from one bank to the other. For the boat ahead, the drop wouldn't have been a big deal. It was considerably larger, and able to take a beating with minimal risk of damage.

However, the raft he and Yasso were riding wasn't designed for such punishment. It was tough, sure, but it had been created to conduct beachhead landings and carry assault troops over calm waters. It wasn't a canoe or kayak, and while it was wider it wasn't as stable.

Bolan withdrew his paddle from the water and dropped it inside the raft. He grabbed both sides of their craft, gripping the handholds sewn into it. He ordered Yasso to do the same, then instructed her to pull the sides toward her as much as she could manage. Their combined strength was enough to lift the sides out of the water.

They accomplished the maneuver just in time.

The raft shot off the drop and sailed almost twenty feet through the air. Bolan's quick thinking paid off. The raft hit the river, but it didn't cause any damage. With the sides of the raft up, married to the fact it was carried by the impetus of natural flow, they skimmed across the river on the same principle as a heavy rock skipped on water. The raft bounced three times before settling onto the surface.

Bolan and Yasso deployed their paddles again and rode out the remaining rush of whitewater.

Over the next half hour or so, the ride became quieter and smoother. Most of the whitewater had diminished, and it appeared they were through the worst. The sound of the boat engine grew louder, and Bolan raised his hand to indicate a decrease in speed.

Yasso quietly put her paddle in the water, following the Executioner's example. The raft slowed until it wasn't moving any faster than the river.

The night sky had cleared. Light filtered down to the river from the moon suspended against a backdrop of brilliant stars.

There was very little wind at that point. A soft breeze shook the firs and saplings that towered above them. Crickets and other animals called from the shadowy stand of trees along the shorelines.

The boat engine died and that puzzled him. He cocked his head to listen, and he could just make out voices.

"What is it, Colonel?"

He shook his head. "I'm not sure. They've stopped for some reason."

"Why do you think—?"

"Shh," he cut in, shaking his head and gesturing for her to be silent.

He listened carefully but couldn't pick out any specific activities. They sat in silence for almost another ten minutes, but nothing more reached his ears with the exception of talking among the terror group.

It was time for a soft probe.

"Stay in the boat," Bolan said. "Got it?"

"I will stay," Yasso whispered. "How long will you be?"

"As long as it takes," he replied.

The Executioner reached into the waterproof sack and withdrew an Uzi. He quietly checked the action while he chambered a round, then stripped out of his webbing. He placed the Uzi near the edge of the raft and slipped his legs over the side. Once he was partially submerged, he rolled onto his stomach and grabbed the Israeli SMG. With the stealth of a soldier born to jungle combat, he eased into the water with hardly a sound.

"If this goes hard," he told Yasso, "you get the hell out of here and you go for assistance."

"Yes, sir," Yasso said. "Be careful."

Nodding curtly, Bolan slithered away from the boat and moved diagonally to the shore until his feet could just touch bottom. His movements were as smooth and silent as an oily rope through a pulley. The soldier knew if he could advance close enough to the boat, he could take it out and the Kahane

Chai terrorists along with it. If the chips sank, they could be recovered.

Bolan hadn't even considered the possibility the chips might have been on the other boat back at Royal Gorge Park. It seemed unlikely, though. The Kahane Chai terrorists seemed intent on getting to their destination. They wouldn't be in such a hurry to report a failure.

No, the ACTEN chips were safely stored on that boat, and Mack Bolan was going to find a way to get to them. First, he would have to deal with the remaining opposition.

The soldier snaked along the riverbank and closed the gap between the boat. He held his Uzi close, muzzle pointed skyward with the action and breech held carefully above the waterline. The Uzi was a dependable and rugged weapon, but it wasn't the most reliable after complete submersion. Some firearms were made for unusual conditions, but the Uzi hadn't been designed for water operations. Most 9 mm weapons tended to jam when exposed to water.

When he was twenty yards off the starboard side, Bolan stopped to carefully assess the situation. There was a little movement on the boat, but it appeared mostly devoid of activity. The soldier could make out a figure who leaned over something that was small and rectangular. He appeared to be talking to the object. A few seconds elapsed before the man spoke again. Suddenly, there was the tinny response coming from the box. It was a radio. So, the Kahane terrorists had stopped to radio their success. Bolan considered the possibility they were scheduled for a pickup, but he quickly dismissed it. According to the map, the operations site was directly accessible from Grey Creek. There would have been no reason to switch to a ground transport. Besides, it would have been impractical in that terrain.

Suddenly, the boat's engine roared to life and the vessel began to pull away.

Bolan raised his weapon but then thought better of it. He was at a tremendous disadvantage if he chose to engage the terrorists now. There would be another opportunity. It was better to let them wait and lead him to their base. Then he could wrap up the whole affair in a single strike.

The Executioner quickly paddled back to the raft.

"Let's go. They're on the move again."

He climbed inside and instructed Yasso to trade places with him. They set off after the boat, both of them paddling for all they were worth. It sounded as if the boat was pulling away. They rounded two bends and Bolan immediately noticed something was wrong. They could hear the boat's engine, but it was nowhere in sight.

As they continued, Bolan noticed a waterway branching off to the right and moving away upstream to the river flow.

"Turn," he ordered Yasso quietly.

The boat swung around, and they began to paddle against the natural flow. Bolan hoped they wouldn't have too far to travel. He was tiring quickly, and he knew Yasso had to be exhausted at this point. Eventually, his second wind would kick in, and he would be good for another twenty-four to thirty-six hours if needed. He hoped it wouldn't drag on that long.

With the conclusion of the mission drawing nearer, Bolan found himself less and less trusting of Yasso. She talked a good game, but there was something else behind all of this trouble. If her theory about Herzhaft not needing the chips *was* true, then that left two options. Yasso had either been duped or she had known and was in on the deal. Either way, she had suffered enough at the hands of the Kahane Chai that he was confident she wouldn't turn on him.

How much was real and how much was subterfuge?

Only time would tell.

ELRAD DAVISCH LED his four men through the thick, dark woods of the San Isabel Forest with only one thing on his mind. Revenge.

Hearing the radio report was good, but it hadn't been the

best news. Apparently, Nahum and the rest of his command staff had been killed. A pair of unknown assailants, one of them a big man who fought like a devil, had nearly wiped out the entire operation force and destroyed one of their boats.

Davisch could scarcely believe his ears as the appointed leader of the escapees had told him of the battle. The reporter wasn't sure who the pursuers had been, but he was confident they had left them far behind. Only nine survived the assault. Thirty men had been part of the operation, and some big, faceless bastard had destroyed more than two-thirds of that force!

The boat had reached the point where the Arkansas merged with Grey Creek. They were now headed up the creek in Davisch's direction. The terrorists were sure they hadn't been followed. Davisch wasn't about to take that chance. If this cowardly demon *was* out there, Davisch would deal with him personally. He would exact retribution for the interference, and the murder of his brothers.

Davisch knew he was disobeying orders by not contacting Mendel, but some things superseded orders. The Americans were soft, flaunting their luxuries and freedoms to those less fortunate. They had never been exposed to the horrors he had known. They went about their daily routines, smug and confident in the personal liberties afforded by money and prestige. Their politicians manipulated the system, and the general population danced to the tune like puppets.

The Jews had seen more persecution than any other group in the history of the world. Countless millions had been tortured, murdered or maimed by forces superior in number but inferior in spirit. His people had been subjected to every form of known terror. His own government had declared the Kach-Kahane Chai movement as terrorists, while the real baby killers and pillagers committed repeated acts of atrocity under their noses.

Davisch believed God had selected them because of this fact, not in spite of it. It was Israel against a Fourth Reich of nations too ignorant or complacent to understand the Jewish plight. One day, those same nations would pay. The machine designed by Herzhaft would make sure of that.

Davisch was fighting for the greater good of his people, and he would use any methods necessary to achieve those ends. No one would shadow the remnants of honorable and courageous Kahane Chai soldiers. Davisch would rally to their cause.

He would destroy the devil once and for all.

THE EXECUTIONER SAW the murky water swirling to the right and just ahead of the raft at the same moment he heard it. The sucking sound of the eddy was subtle, barely audible, but it seemed like thunder in Bolan's ears.

"Whirlpool," he said. "A large one."

"What do we do?" Yasso asked, the panic evident in her tone.

"Paddle toward that side," he replied.

The two began to fight against the draw of water that was increasing at a furious pace.

Bolan pushed his paddle against the current, trying to force the back of the raft away from the danger zone, but he had spotted the eddy a moment too late. He could hear Yasso wheezing with exertion, and he could see the obvious tension as she flailed with her paddle.

"Large strokes," he instructed her. "Give it all you have."

For a moment, it seemed as if the raft was pulling away, but Bolan knew they were only delaying the inevitable. The eddy was apparently large enough to pull them in, but somehow the larger boat they had been chasing escaped unharmed. The engine and large pontoons on the craft had probably displaced enough of the water to leave the eddy ineffective against its superior weight and speed.

Bolan looked behind him and judged the distance from the eddy to the creek bank was probably about ten feet. He could make the jump, but he wasn't sure about Yasso. She would have to bail now if she had any chance of surviving.

"You need to get out of here," Bolan said calmly.

"No!" she countered. "I will not leave."

"Dammit, lady, don't argue with me. Take the equipment and get out. *Now.*"

Yasso turned back and looked at him with a surprised expression. He stared back at her, and he could see she realized he was serious. The raft would provide enough of a draw to block the suction in front of the helm. The Mossad agent would be able to get out and swim to shore before the shearing forces drew the raft in.

Bolan knew he would have to wait until the last second to get out. If he didn't escape, Yasso would at least have the equipment and means necessary to find the Kahane Chai and end the problem. He wasn't about to let her join the ranks of his ghosts. He had enough blood on his hands.

Yasso smiled. "I wish you well, Colonel Pollock. You have been a valued ally."

"That's touching," Bolan replied, fighting the eddy with every bit of reserve strength he could muster. "Now move it."

Yasso quickly untied the rucksack and slung it behind her. She wrapped the only remaining strap around her waist, looped it through the top strap and tied a knot around it. Without looking back at Bolan, she knelt on the front of the raft and dived into the dark waters.

Once she had advanced a few yards, Bolan began to ease his resistance. He forced the raft into a tight circle until the nose was pointed directly at the eddy. With nothing more to hold it back, the soldier watched the raft rush forward as he reached down and grasped the wrapped M-16.

His timing would have to be perfect. If he jumped too soon, he'd fall short of the bank and be dragged into a watery grave. If he jumped too late, the raft would collapse and trap him inside. Neither choice presented a terribly appealing option, and the Executioner knew he had no choice but to do it once and do it right.

He did.

Bolan landed prone on the shore, with only the lower part of his legs splashing into the water. He quickly got to his feet and turned just in time to see Yasso emerge onto the opposite bank. She rose and waved at him, although he could barely discern her in the darkness. She appeared unhurt.

By the time the soldier looked down at the eddy, the raft was gone. The water began to shimmer and gurgle, and suddenly the swirling energies disappeared, leaving only timid ripples in their wake. The raft had probably plugged the sinkhole at the bottom of the creek. The Executioner was actually perplexed by the whole thing. Creek eddies weren't typically powerful, because creek beds usually weren't that deep.

Yeah, it had been damn close.

Bolan unwrapped the M-16 and quickly donned his fatigue shirt. He then gestured with his arm, indicating that Yasso should meet him farther up the bank. He would wait for an opportunity to cross over where it was safe. Once he was sure she had understood his intentions, the soldier turned and began negotiating the bank.

He stopped often, crouching to listen and probe the mysterious and shadowy woods with keen eyes. He kept an eye on the opposing shore and watched for signs of regular movement. Minutes would pass in some places as he waited for Yasso to match his pace. Every so often, Bolan would step out of the wood line and signal that he was still there. She would follow the example, and then they would move on.

They had advanced about three hundred yards when Bolan decided to inspect the creek on the chance he might be able to cross. He exited the wood line and knelt. The water was still, and the Executioner listened intently for the sound of hazards. There was no swirling water, no sounding of rushing tides. Nothing but a gentle babble sounded farther upstream, which indicated the creek depth had decreased. Bolan signaled to Yasso and took a step into the creek.

He froze at the sound of movement behind him.

14

Bolan heard them before he saw them. It was more difficult for a group of men moving through thick woods to hear a single opponent than in a one-on-one situation. He turned and glanced in Yasso's direction. She noticed his sudden change in posture and slowly slipped into the wood line.

The soldier returned his attention to the enemy. He probed the darkness, every sense on full alert. The sound of a branch being pushed aside gave him the general location and angle of approach. Slowly, one shadowy form upon another emerged through a clearing in the trees. Bolan made a quick count. Five.

And they looked heavily armed.

He still had the advantage. If he were going to seize it, he would have to allow them to draw closer. One of the assets of a good warrior was patience. If it wasn't exercised with due regard, and coupled with an ability to improvise and adapt to an ever changing situation, the hunter could quickly become the prey. It was a rare occurrence for the Executioner to be the quarry—he'd developed that sense of timing that kept him on the offensive and his enemy off guard.

Bolan watched with interest. A burly giant led the group. He moved with surprising stealth for his girth, but he didn't appear accustomed to such terrain. The soldier could smell his enemy. One of them was smoking, they were walking in single file and they were clustered entirely too close to one another.

He waited until the group passed his position before launching his assault.

The Executioner rose from the creek bed, noiselessly stepped next to a tree for cover and lined the sights of the M-16 on the center man.

The first burst struck the target dead center. The man's body flipped through the air and crashed into dense foliage a few feet from his comrades.

Bolan sighted on the man immediately to the front of the first target before the patrol had time to react. He closed one eye, took a deep breath, let half out and squeezed the trigger. Three rounds of 5.56 mm ball ammunition slammed home, punching holes in the man's chest as the remaining trio dived for cover. The Kahane Chai terrorist connected with a nearby tree and slid to the forest floor.

The Executioner changed position, sprinting in a beeline to another thick pine. The hardmen on the ground opened up with their Galil rifles on full auto, struggling to ascertain the position of their target. Their aim was atrocious, and they sent a hail of bullets in a direction nowhere near Bolan's position.

The soldier flipped up the leaf sight on the M-203 and prepared to open fire. He aimed for the enemy's approximate position as their autofire died down under the screams of the apparent leader. He decided on a good level and pulled the launcher's trigger.

The firing pin fell with a dull click.

Movement sounded through the underbrush and Bolan threw himself to the ground in time to avoid a fresh barrage from the three assault rifles. The noise had given away his position. He rolled four times under the cover of the deafening fire and came up on one knee on the group's right flank. One of the muzzle-flashes from the Galils was visible through the underbrush. Bolan raised the M-16 to his shoulder and sighted just down and to the left, adjusting for muzzle rise.

He opened up on the position with sustained fire.

Screams of agony echoed in his ears as the enemy's autofire

died. Bolan waited a moment until he heard nothing more. He let a full minute pass, waiting for even the slightest sounds of life or movement. Nothing.

The warrior rose and carefully advanced through the brush. He came upon two bodies and studied them a moment.

As Bolan realized that there was one missing, the lone survivor of the squad made his presence known. He raced through the brush screaming like a wild man, the bullet-shattered Galil clutched in his hands and positioned over his left shoulder. The remaining, jagged pieces of the rifle's wooden stock were testament to his near demise. The right side of the man's face was filled with large cuts where the stock had exploded under Bolan's fire. Blood poured from the wounds and soaked the front of the man's desert fatigues.

It was the hulking man who had been on point. He swung his Galil in a crushing arc toward Bolan's face. The warrior ducked back in time to avoid permanent disfigurement, but the sharp stock remnant rammed into his right shoulder and pierced the skin. His opponent yanked the weapon out and swung it over his head, his face contorted with killing frenzy.

The Executioner fought the pain, clearing his mind and ducking the wild swing. His enemy was fighting on pure rage and adrenaline, and Bolan knew cunning and speed were his best allies at this point.

The attacker stopped the swing short and reversed its direction before Bolan could reach for his knife. In close combat, he didn't stand a chance of shooting the man with the bulky rifle. He swung the stock up and deflected the vicious assault. The plastic forward handgrip of his M-16 shattered under the impact, pieces of plastic flying in every direction.

Bolan swung the stock down and into the big man's groin. The terrorist screamed in agony as his adversary stomped his boot against a knee. Bones and cartilage snapped audibly above the man's wail. The leg gave out under the hardman, and he dropped onto his back.

The Executioner was on him, clearing his knife from its

sheath. He swung toward the man's chest, but his opponent caught Bolan's wrist and stopped the cold steel blade mere inches from his chest. The soldier fought against the tremendous grip on his wrist, attempting to twist free at the weakest point between the man's thumb and forefinger. His enemy nearly turned the blade on Bolan, and the warrior slammed a knee into the man's groin. He immediately followed that with repetitious hammer blows to the terrorist's chest.

The man fought back ferociously and used his free hand to punch Bolan in the jaw. His ham-sized fist nearly caved in the left side of the Executioner's face, and the soldier almost lapsed into unconsciousness when a loud crack rolled up his jaw and into his ears.

Bolan sat up and yanked his wrist back, locking his opponent's arm. He started to twist his body to the left to brace the elbow against his stomach, but the bigger man used the split-second delay to roll him onto his back, and the terrorist landed with both knees to one side of Bolan's hips. In the midst of the roll, the knife was buried into the man's left arm.

The terrorist's shock was the diversion Bolan needed.

He threw one leg high in the air, wrapped his thigh around the giant's neck, then sat up, straining leg muscles to pin his opponent to the ground. He continued to apply pressure, scissoring the man's neck between his legs. The hardman's choked whispers signaled imminent victory.

The terrorist reached up and pulled the knife from his arm in a last-ditch effort for survival. He raised the blade to bury it in Bolan's thigh, but his movements served only to facilitate a tighter hold. The sound of vertebrae snapping in the man's neck resounded with unquestionable finality. The knife slipped from numb fingers as all the signals between brain and body ceased.

The odors of bowel and bladder releasing stung Bolan's nostrils as the man let out a final, gurgled sigh.

The Executioner released the giant and lay on his back, panting with exhaustion. Beads of cold sweat ran down his face and neck. The fight had lasted under a minute, but Bolan felt as if a lifetime had passed. His enemy was strong and fearless, a deadly combination that the soldier knew all too well.

Bolan looked at his shoulder, reminded of the injury as a fresh wave of pain washed over him. He was nauseated and close to losing consciousness. He needed food and rest, but neither of those seemed near. There was still an army of Kahane Chai terrorists to be dealt with out there somewhere.

By his calculations, the numbers were running down.

"I'VE ABOUT HAD IT," Bolan muttered.

He watched Yasso as she patched his arm with small, delicate hands, her brows furrowed in concentration. Every so often, she would look at the Executioner and study him. It was almost like she were seeing someone from the past. A ghost perhaps? Maybe a former lover or friend? Bolan had the nagging sense that when Yasso looked at him, she was seeing someone else.

He could relate to that. In some respects, Yasso reminded him of his sister—the "other woman" he'd mentioned earlier. Cindy didn't cross Bolan's mind often. When she did, it was usually because something would trigger some long-dead emotion. Sometimes, it was the smell of certain perfumes, a shy and innocent face, an inquisitive nature or a spirited view toward life.

Yasso had all of these traits, and the soldier felt hard-pressed to keep his emotion in check. Perhaps he was tired or feeling the effects of the numbing antiseptic included in their pack's first-aid kit. Either way, it had been a long time ago.

Yeah, a very long time ago.

"We have nothing to prevent infection," Yasso said. She watched him expectantly with her dark brown eyes. "You will probably need antibiotics, and there are a couple shards of wood in there I wouldn't dare try to remove."

"I've had worse," Bolan murmured. "Actually, that wood will minimize the bleeding. It looks good. Thanks."

Yasso only nodded.

The Executioner rose from his place on their downed log and pulled the trousers from the ALICE pack. He slid into them, working them over his boots and boxers, then donned his webbing. Bolan had left the broken M-16 behind and stripped the weapon of the M-203. The buffer spring in the stock of the M-16 dampened much of the kick from the grenade launcher, but it wasn't impossible to use separate from the rifle.

He also restocked his ammo pouches with fresh clips for the two Galils that he'd stripped from the terrorist squad.

"What do we do now, Colonel?" Yasso asked tiredly. She, too, had dressed.

Bolan walked back to her and produced a topographical map that he'd found on the giant. He switched on his flashlight and studied the map carefully. For a moment, he was puzzled. He looked up and let himself take in the immediate terrain. When his gaze finally returned to the map, he was shaking his head.

"Well, that boat is long gone."

"Do you know where we are?"

"No," Bolan said, "but I know where we aren't." He pointed to the map and indicated a general direction. "That's magnetic north."

The soldier pulled the tritium compass from his pocket and checked their bearings. Realistically, he knew it wasn't necessary. All they really had to do was follow Grey Creek, but he wasn't willing to take chances. He couldn't be sure the map was accurate. Moreover, the darkness added complications. There was no way to accurately judge the distance they still had to cover, but the Executioner guessed it was at least a thousand yards, and possibly farther.

"I am not sure I can go on," Yasso murmured. "I am so tired, Colonel."

Bolan glanced at his watch and saw it was nearly 0300 hours. It wouldn't do them any good to push themselves until they dropped. He had to admit he was tired himself. They would need rest at some point, and the warrior didn't foresee there would be further resistance.

If there were going to be a showdown, it would be on the Kahane Chai's home turf.

"All right," he agreed, looking at her with concern. "I think we can afford an hour, maybe two...but no more. Fair enough?"

"Yes. Thank you."

"I'll wake us up when it's time to leave."

He noticed her grab her shoulders and shiver. He took off his shirt top and sat down with his back to the log. He gestured for her to sit next to him, and she practically surged into his embrace. She laid her head on his chest, and he wrapped his arms around her as he positioned the shirt top over them as a makeshift blanket. The soft pattern of her breathing was almost intoxicating as she rested her hands on his forearms. He dwarfed her in size, his massive frame encircling her like a cocoon of protection.

Yasso let out a satisfied sigh before she drifted to sleep almost immediately.

Bolan closed his eyes, but kept his senses focused on the surroundings. He would be ready for any threat that suddenly presented itself. He would protect Yasso, sure, but he would also protect the interests of his country. It was only a matter of time until they found the operations site.

Then he would cut out the heart of the Kahane Chai.

AS DAWN CREPT over the horizon, Bolan's eyes snapped open.

It was time to move out.

He gently shook Yasso to wake her. She lifted her head from his chest, yawned and rubbed her eyes. Crickets chirped in the underbrush, interspersed by the occasional croak of a concealed bullfrog perched somewhere near the bank of the creek. Birds sang their morning tunes in the trees far above the pair.

Yasso got to her feet, stretched and quickly fussed with her dark hair.

Bolan noticed her watching him as he worked the soreness from his injured shoulder. He had a dry, pasty feeling in his mouth, and it hurt to move his jaw. Despite his injuries, he was no worse for the wear. The two-hour nap had revived him enough that he figured he could function. He'd gain his second wind as they advanced toward the Kahane Chai's operation site.

Bolan got to his feet and handed the ALICE pack to Yasso. She took the rucksack without complaint. There was no way the strap would fit around the Executioner's large frame. He would have to carry the Galil with the M-203, as well as his Uzi, webbing, spare ammo clips and the Desert Eagle. The pack was light and Yasso didn't appear to mind.

They began to hike through the woods with Bolan on point.

The soldier's eyes roved the furtive nooks and crannies of the surrounding forest.

The arrival of daylight would present as many new problems as it would advantages. They could move faster through the rugged terrain now, but they were also more visible to the enemy. If they arrived at their destination before the Kahane Chai could escape with the chips, Bolan would then face the problem of conducting a reconnaissance without the benefit of darkness. Both he and Yasso would be easier targets, especially when they considered that the Kahane likely outnumbered them fifteen to one.

Yasso pressed close to the Executioner. "How far do you think we will have to go?"

"I'm not sure. Maybe a mile."

"We are running out of time, aren't we?"

"Yeah."

It was the truth. Without outside assistance, the soldier had his work cut out for him. He knew Yasso was still convinced there was a way to save the computer technology. Bolan felt otherwise, but he didn't see a need to tell her that. He would evaluate the situation for what it was worth, and make the appropriate decision when the time came.

Besides, the ACTEN chips were only a secondary concern. The mission now hinged upon destroying the Kahane Chai. The packaging made the chips almost impervious to outside means of sabotage. In a way, the American government had made a crucial error on that count. The very steps they had taken to secure the chips could now prove to be their ultimate demise.

It didn't matter. If the Executioner could stop the Kahane terror group before they were able to leave the country, whether or not the chips survived would become a moot point.

There were two other concerns that plagued Bolan more. One of them was Ilia Yasso. He didn't have any real reason to mistrust her, but he couldn't seem to drive away the deception he sensed on her part. She acted like someone with a personal agenda—something that existed beyond the outward appearance. She had fought beside him and tended to his wounds. She seemed dedicated to help him accomplish the mission, even if it meant compromising her mission. It wasn't outright treachery. He couldn't put his finger on a subtle deceit, so he would have to watch for her to make her move.

Bolan's second concern centered on Baram Herzhaft. If the Israeli scientist had struck a deal with the Kahane Chai to play two ends against the middle, the danger wouldn't necessarily die with the elimination of the terrorists. Both the U.S. and Israel could still be vulnerable. Herzhaft might simply dole out the ACTEN device to the highest bidder. He could advertise his machine on the black market, and drop it in the laps of another organization even more dangerous than the Kach-Kahane movement.

Even if the Executioner succeeded in destroying the Kahane Chai, he would still have to deal with Herzhaft. It was one more thing to complicate the situation. He pushed it aside and focused his attention back to the present.

They had been marching through the forest for nearly an hour when the sounds of voices and machinery stopped Bolan in his tracks. He raised his hand as he crouched. Yasso settled quietly to the ground and crept up to his position. She looked at him, an inquiring expression on her face, and he pointed to an area on the far side of the creek.

She nodded when the flash of sunlight on metal caught her eye. It was the boat the Kahane had used to transport the chips. The craft rocked gently in the creek bed, tethered to the shore. Troops soon became apparent through the dense foliage. Some of the Kahane Chai terrorists hauled equipment and loaded it into the rear of a C-141 cargo plane, while others struck tents and packed gear.

Bolan watched the activity for a moment and nodded silently. This confirmed his worst nightmare.

"They're going to fly the chips out of here," he whispered grimly.

"I do not understand," Yasso replied with a shake of her head. "Why have they gone to so much trouble, Colonel?"

"They wouldn't have been able to just lift the chips out from under the Army's nose," Bolan explained. "Somehow, they managed to get that plane into American airspace. They probably knew the flight plan of the real transport, and now they're just following it."

"I think I am beginning to understand. They have simply duplicated your government's original plan to deliver the chips to Israel."

Bolan nodded. "It wouldn't arouse any suspicions, since the personnel on Fort Carson didn't know Jacoby's agenda. It cinches our theory they engineered some sort of disaster at Carson, and then left without anyone being the wiser."

"So the United States Army believes we are still on the base?"

"Probably."

"Won't your radar systems detect the plane in American airspace?"

"I'm sure someone sold them the authorization code to transmit if they're questioned, as well as the flight plan. It was probably that Lieutenant Ford from Team Bravo. That's why they're pushing the timetable."

"Please explain," Yasso said.

"It's simple. This mission was supposed to be top secret. That means congressional authority, probably under an executive order. Nobody's going to question that, particularly if the operation is proceeding as planned."

"By the time your government realizes what has happened," Yasso replied, her eyes widening, "it will be too late."

"Exactly."

"We cannot allow them to leave with the ACTEN chips, Colonel."

"Don't worry about that," Bolan said grimly. "They're not going anywhere."

15

Major Malcolm Dunham surveyed the carnage and death with horror.

The smell of cordite, blood and destruction seemed odd in the tranquil beauty of a Colorado sunrise. The pink-and-red-orange hues of dawn cast unusual shades on the congealed blood that had run freely from the dead. The bodies of the executed SF commandos lay prone in the courtyard, mingled with the scattered remains of unidentified men in desert fatigues. Equipment was strewed across the entire training site— grenades, crates, a spent LAW—and large parts of some of the village houses were nothing more than crumbling hovels.

The morning light reflected off the brass casings from spent shells, some of which were piled in certain areas. There had been a battle here of epic proportions. Colonel Jacoby's body was found near a lone Quonset hut. The building was devoid of vehicles, and the darkened, battle-scarred remains of an M2A2 Bradley sat on the outskirts of the mock village.

The bodies of more Green Berets were found inside some of the houses. The soldiers' throats were cut with thin, deep lines, which indicated they had been the victims of wire garrotes. The huts the group had used for billets were empty.

The remains of Captain Ralston were also among the dead, and preliminary reports indicated he'd been blown to bits by a grenade.

What the hell had he been running from?

As investigators from the MP corps and CID perused the

grounds, Dunham watched them with tired eyes. When General Wasserman had instructed Lieutenant Asher to find Jacoby, he never imagined the search would end like this. The thing that bothered Dunham most was the missing computer technology Jacoby was supposed to have escorted to Israel.

The trucks Jacoby had requisitioned were also gone. All of the gates swore they hadn't checked out Jacoby's group, and it didn't take Dunham long to discover why. While on his roving patrol, he found the holes cut in a fence line on the western perimeter of the post.

The perpetrators behind this vicious attack had slipped in and out undetected during the emergency.

Carson was still on total lockdown. The Army wasn't any closer to discovering the reason for the mayhem that appeared to stem from computer problems. The Pentagon was screaming for assistance, and word had it that even the President and Congress were involved now. The civilian press and television news crews were practically climbing the walls. Concerned family members of military personnel stationed at the post had nearly overrun the front gates in an attempt to get some answers about the nature and duration of the emergency.

Major General Wasserman apparently didn't give a damn. Fort Carson was *his* post, and he wasn't about to let the public take control. Dunham could only admire his commanding officer for that.

As it was, communications were still down. Field lines had been strung between major areas on the post, and they were making use of satellite-powered cellular telephones air dropped by a crew from Peterson. Dunham was handling the majority of inquiries and public-relations issues.

Technicians had been working on the computer problem all night, but nothing they tried seemed to work. In most cases, they couldn't even get the operating systems or displays to work. It would be difficult to determine the source of the trouble if they couldn't access basic functions. Earlier that morning, one of the technicians managed to restore power to the computers at the post headquarters building.

Crews rushed to his aid and immediately began to install encryption programs to backtrack system files and troubleshoot any possible hardware conflicts. File fragments had been detected, which was a clear indicator of a virus, according to the experts.

There were a ton of questions and no answers, and this fact frustrated Dunham. One thing was certain—the incident here and the shutdown of the post were related. There was no longer a question in General Wasserman's mind about that fact. It was obvious that the entire incident was the work of an outside force. If the present debacle was any indication, this new and faceless enemy was well trained and extremely hostile.

Given the chance, Dunham meant to deal with the threat.

He was a stalwart black man in his late thirties with a bald head and large, heavy-lidded eyes. He carried an air of authority wherever he went, and chewed constantly on an unlit cigar. It had become almost a trademark for the post XO. Dunham commanded respect, and Wasserman considered him to be one of the finest officers in the U.S. Army.

"Sir?" Dunham called. He stood near Wasserman's command vehicle and held a satellite phone receiver to his ear.

Wasserman turned from where he'd been speaking with a CID officer and walked to where Dunham waited.

"What is it, Major?" Wasserman demanded.

"There's a priority call coming in," Dunham replied. He handed the receiver to Wasserman and quietly added, "It's the President, sir."

Wasserman clicked his heels as he snatched the receiver. "Yes, Mr. President, this is Major General Donald Wasserman, Fort Carson headquarters."

There was a pause, and Dunham watched Wasserman with eager expectation.

"No, sir, we haven't determined the problem." There was

another lapse. "Yes, sir, we've been working on it all night. I have just discovered Colonel Jacoby's mission was compromised, and the ACTEN technology has been stolen from the post."

Wasserman listened carefully. He held the phone away from his ear during a point where Dunham could hear the commander in chief yelling. Finally, he became calm and issued a veritable list of orders that Wasserman related to Dunham as they were given.

Dunham immediately wrote them down word for word.

"No, sir, we have no idea who's behind the penetration," Wasserman replied. "I beg your pardon, sir? No, the entire installation is still locked down, sir. We have no radar systems, and I cannot authorize any aircraft to leave the post. I am simply enacting the emergency powers authorized under such—"

Wasserman broke off as the President buzzed an interjection.

"If you order me to do it, Mr. President, I'll obey the order," Wasserman finally said. "However, I would like it on record the order was obeyed under protest." A pause. "No, sir, I am only concerned with the safety and welfare of the soldiers under my command."

Wasserman cut another protest and listened, nodding occasionally.

"Yes, sir, I will expect them," he replied. "I hope so, and thank you very much, Mr. President."

Wasserman disconnected the call, and Dunham looked at him expectantly.

"He's not happy, Malcolm," Wasserman told him. "He's not happy at all. He said he wants us to maintain tight security and wait for this special team that's arriving within thirty minutes. They're going to land by jet at the airfield, so we had best get over there immediately."

"Did he say what this special team intends to do, sir?" Dunham asked.

"I don't know. I guess we'll find out soon enough."

HAL BROGNOLA WATCHED as Jack Grimaldi piloted the VC-20 Gulfstream jet into a steep bank, then level off and begin his descent.

He leaned forward in his seat and tried to determine exactly what Grimaldi intended to use as a guide. According to their intelligence, Fort Carson had neither radar nor electricity, so there would be no runway lights, directional beacons or homing signals. Moreover, Grimaldi would have to set the jet down by sight, a difficult task for an instrument-rated pilot in an instrument-rated aircraft.

Brognola finally sat back and let out a nervous sigh. He trusted Grimaldi implicitly. The man's skills went back to the earliest days of Striker's wars against the Mafia. Even before that time, Grimaldi had shown his piloting talents in the jungle hellgrounds of Vietnam.

Since his redemption from the Mob, Grimaldi had served Stony Man with distinction. There was a special place in the veteran's heart for the big guy in black. He cared about Bolan as much as any of them did. If Striker's life might hinge upon a successful landing, Grimaldi would put that bird down in a landing zone no larger than a quarter with room to spare.

Grimaldi held up a pair of fingers to indicate there were two minutes to touchdown.

Brognola grunted and fastened his seat belt. He turned to study Kurtzman, who sat nearby in his wheelchair, but the Stony Man computer whiz didn't meet his eye. The man was furiously typing at a laptop keyboard, his eyes scanning the information that rolled across the screen. Behind those eyes, the mind was probably moving as quickly as the machine, and Brognola chose not to interrupt him.

Brognola glanced at another passenger aboard the plane, but there was no admiration in this look.

Dr. Baram Herzhaft's haggard face stared back at him with an empty expression. Herzhaft knew what was at stake—at least he thought he did. Brognola could find little reason to sympathize with the man. He was a traitor to Israel and the United States. If Herzhaft was shot for his actions, Brognola would be hard-pressed to feel sorry for him. The most troubling thing was the fact that a brilliant and inventive man was left a shell because he'd allowed himself to be duped by a ruthless band of thugs.

If they could set things right, at least Herzhaft would find some solace in that.

Barbara Price had remained at the Farm, collating information as it came in. She'd telephoned with troubling news about a gun battle that had occurred just outside Cañon City, Colorado. While Brognola might have shrugged it off as coincidence, there was no mistaking the signature marks of a Bolan effect. Undoubtedly, Striker was on the move.

The reports detailed involvement of dead men wearing desert camouflage uniforms, and the flaming wreckage of two vehicles. More information poured in about complaints of gunfire at Royal Gorge Park, a tourist attraction located near the original fight. Additional bodies had apparently been found there, and the police were completely baffled.

The information all pointed to the Executioner, but Brognola could not act on that alone. Striker could take care of himself. The President was more concerned with the emergency at Fort Carson, and deservedly so. The ACTEN device was important, but that wasn't the President's chief aim. They were bordering on a national incident, and the sooner the Army could get things under control, the sooner things could return to normal and Brognola could then get to the bottom of the Kahane Chai connection.

Grimaldi landed at the post airfield without a hitch.

Brognola led his small entourage down the boarding ramp and was greeted by Major General Donald Wasserman. Brognola had read the post commander's file during the trip to Fort Carson. The man had an impeccable record, and he couldn't have asked for a better liaison. Wasserman's approach to no-

nonsense leadership might be a hurdle, but Brognola was acting on the authority of the White House.

He'd set the general straight if Wasserman got out of line.

"Mr. Brognola, it's a pleasure," Wasserman said, stepping forward and offering his hand. "Welcome to Fort Carson."

"Thank you, General." Brognola gestured to Kurtzman. "This is Mr. Kershner, and I think you're going to be rather glad to see him."

"Oh?" Wasserman raised his eyebrows and gazed at Kurtzman with interest. "I hope you can help us, sir."

"I'll do my best, General," Kurtzman replied easily.

The two men shook hands.

Brognola didn't bother to introduce Herzhaft, and Wasserman didn't ask. They walked toward a white government van that served as a staff vehicle. A second Army officer, this one black and bald, with a cigar clenched in his teeth, opened the door for Wasserman as the men approached.

"This is my executive officer, Major Malcolm Dunham," the general said before climbing into the front seat of the sedan.

The men exchanged handshakes around. Two MPs lifted Kurtzman into the van, wheelchair and all, while Brognola took a forward seat immediately behind the cab. Dunham and Herzhaft took the rearmost seat, and soon the entire group was riding toward the post headquarters.

Brognola opened the conversation.

"I assume the President has contacted you, since you were expecting us, General."

"Yes, sir, he did," Wasserman replied congenially. "I must admit, I wasn't happy with the idea. I've restricted all aircraft or other vehicle movement until this situation is under control."

"I can sympathize with your situation," Brognola acquiesced. "Nevertheless, I'm certain we can help you resolve this matter. It doesn't matter to me who takes the credit, so let's get that out of the way right now. Fair enough?"

Wasserman turned and stared at Brognola with an expression of surprise. The Stony Man leader could tell the officer had viewed their interference as nothing but glory grabbing, but Brognola had no such ambitions. There were other things that needed attention, and if they could get the post up and strong enough to stand on its own feet, it wouldn't be soon enough to suit him.

"Go on," Wasserman prodded, although there was still a cautious tone in his voice.

"There are two important elements we're here to address. How to restore the function of Fort Carson, and how to find out where the perpetrators have gone."

"Unfortunately, I don't have answers to either of those questions, Mr. Brognola," Wasserman interjected.

"We may have answers to both. I'll first need to speak with Lieutenant Colonel Jacoby."

A grim quiet fell over Wasserman, and alarms began to sound in Brognola's head. He couldn't shake the sudden sensation that something had gone terribly wrong at Fort Carson, and he almost couldn't ask the next question.

"Is he dead?"

Wasserman nodded and Brognola shook his head with disbelief.

"How did it happen?" he asked.

"We're not sure," Wasserman said, "but it would appear his team was ambushed. We found the bodies at the training site a few hours ago. Dunham discovered someone had penetrated the western perimeter, and unfortunately they managed to wipe out our people and steal the computer technology."

Wasserman's statement confirmed everything Herzhaft had told him. The Kahane Chai had obviously transported the chips to Cañon City, or some place near it anyway, and Bolan was probably hot on their trail. It had all come together for him, and Brognola was ready to lend assistance any way he could.

"If it's all the same to you, General," Brognola ventured,

"I'm going to need your authorization to mobilize a task force. I believe we may know where the enemy who killed Jacoby and his men are located."

"I'm sorry, Mr. Brognola, but I can't allow that," Wasserman replied hesitantly. "I know I'm supposed to cooperate with you, and I'm sure you could serve my head on a platter at the Pentagon. However, and I told the President this, I cannot risk any more lives. I have thousands of troops on this post, not to mention all of the support staff. I cannot spare the equipment or the manpower unless we can shut this thing down here and now."

Brognola couldn't argue with him. Wasserman was right. Despite how he felt about Bolan's life, there were more lives at stake. Striker wouldn't have wanted Stony Man to sacrifice everything just to save one man. The needs of innocent people across the region were of much greater importance, as was the security of a nation. Bolan wouldn't have risked less or asked more for any other reason, and Brognola knew he would have to accept that.

The Executioner could take care of himself.

"Okay, General," Brognola finally replied, "we'll play it your way."

"Thank you."

"What exactly has happened to the post computer system and utilities?" Dunham jumped in. "Do you have any idea?"

"We're sure we know exactly what's wrong, Major," Kurtzman replied. "I'd be willing to bet you have partial power restored. Maybe you're even using supplemental or auxiliary systems. A generator perhaps?"

"Yes," Dunham said with genuine surprise. "How did you know that?"

"That's not all," Kurtzman beamed. "I would also venture to guess your computer people are finding fragments of files and programs through the system, and they're probably telling you it's this huge virus."

"That's astounding!"

"Not really, Major. The very thing your people are doing is destroying the system. They might think they're cleaning things out, but they're eliminating files and programs and a whole mess of other vital information we'll need to restore the network. I hope you have backups."

"We'll provide you with everything we can," Dunham said.

"General Wasserman," Brognola said, "I have a proposition."

"I'm listening."

"If my team can get your systems back online, will you agree to release some aircraft and soldiers for my discretionary use?"

"Mr. Brognola," Wasserman boomed, "if you can do that, I'll give you the whole damned Third Brigade Combat Team if you want it."

"It's a deal, General."

AARON KURTZMAN SAT in front of the terminal in Wasserman's office and plugged his laptop system into the back of the computer.

All power had been routed to the headquarters building, and the entire building was alive with personnel and computer technicians. Fort Carson shared a huge networking system, and Kurtzman knew what he did there would affect everything. They would have one chance to get it right, and the possibility existed that success or failure would determine Mack Bolan's demise. Kurtzman pushed the thought from his mind. The big guy made his own destiny, and the Stony Man computer expert was there to help him run the numbers.

Herzhaft sat next to Kurtzman and began to guide him through the process. The air was charged with excitement, and it rippled through the headquarters staff like electricity. This added to the tension, but it also increased Kurtzman's efficiency. He operated best under pressure and deadlines. This was what he lived for; it was the reason he chose to survive the ordeal that had paralyzed him for life.

"Okay," Herzhaft said calmly. "The first step will be to defragment the files so that you can read each cluster individually."

"That's going to take some time."

"Yes, especially since you must restore the system files first."

"Okay," Kurtzman muttered.

The Stony Man computer wizard began to tap at the keyboard with furious purpose. They were going to have to beat the clock on this one. Kurtzman forced every other thought from his mind as he began to order the system to defragment the files using encryption codes from the twin 128-bit processors within his laptop.

As the system started to defragment, the terminal screen flickered a few times, then a blue background appeared covered with unreadable black-and-gray characters. It was working. Kurtzman looked at his laptop screen as the device signal began to buzz for attention.

"Okay, I'm in the system, Doctor," Kurtzman said. "According to the information here, there are 786,000 files throughout the network. Of those, more than two hundred thousand are system files."

"Can you isolate them from the remaining files?" Herzhaft asked.

"I think so, but I'll have to access each individual drive to do it."

Herzhaft shrugged and looked at Kurtzman sympathetically. "I understand, but that is the only way to reverse the process."

"Maybe not," he replied on afterthought.

"You have a suggestion?"

"No, Doctor," Kurtzman said with a smile. "I have a solution."

16

Mack Bolan pressed himself deeper beneath the undergrowth.

He crawled to a position near the bank of Grey Creek and settled for a spot that would afford him a view of the Kahane Chai encampment. The soldier lifted the field binoculars to his eyes and moved them along the operations area. He marked a gray tent on the far side of the camp, nestled among natural cover near a wood line.

The hum of generators was still apparent under the din of moving equipment.

On a makeshift airstrip in the distance, Bolan adjusted the focus knob for a closer look at the plane. It was definitely an American-made C-141, its tail ramp lowered to allow continuous loading of the equipment. Six armed guards encircled the ramp, providing security as another half-dozen Kahane terrorists loaded plain, unmarked crates. Bolan shifted his view to the cockpit, but he couldn't make out any shadows inside.

Beside the twelve guards at the plane, the Executioner counted at least another ten to fifteen spread throughout the remainder of the operations area. Some were sitting near the lone tent, while others walked the wood line or scattered themselves along the shore.

Bolan had instructed Yasso to remain hidden farther back. He wanted to probe the area and get a feel for the resistance they might encounter. Actually, *he* would encounter the resistance. He had other plans for Yasso, and they involved destroying the C-141.

The soldier figured he had two options.

The first would have been to launch the remaining grenades into the plane, which would effectively neutralize the Kahane Chai's plans. With that accomplished, he could pick off as many as possible before they escaped, and then contact Stony Man. Able Team or Phoenix Force could easily track the rest of them.

It wasn't a bad plan, but it put the general population at risk. He couldn't afford to allow the Kahane Chai to escape. Not only was it likely the terrorists would seek vengeance, but also they would take their aggressions out on innocent bystanders, and Bolan wouldn't let that happen.

The second option presented a more realistic effort, considering the situation. If the Executioner could draw the terrorists into the woods, he might be able to destroy them in small groups. While he kept the terrorists busy, Yasso could attempt to penetrate the camp and recover the chips. This would satisfy a dual purpose, and decrease the risks to her considerably.

Just because the beautiful Mossad agent knew the dangers and was willing to shoulder her share of them didn't give Bolan the right to throw away her life unnecessarily. She was as much a victim and unwilling participant in the Kahane Chai's deceptions as Jacoby had been.

That left only one issue—how to create the diversion he needed. He studied the surrounding area and decided the best angle of approach would be from the other side. Drawing the Kahane across the creek was neither realistic nor practical. Even given that the creek was shallow, Bolan knew he couldn't draw a sufficient number across.

He lowered the binoculars and looked around the camp. The flash of the boat caught his peripheral vision, and he turned to look at it. At first, he experienced a blank, but then it hit him. If he could get on board and turn the boat around, he could make it appear as if he were trying to escape. They would more than likely send a pursuit party. It was worth a try.

With his plan firmly decided, Bolan turned and headed toward where he had left Yasso.

It was time for action.

JURRE MENDEL sat inside the tent and wondered what had happened to Davisch and his men. He wondered why they hadn't made a report since their radio contact with the boat, and he wondered why the boat team had missed the squad. Who had interfered with the operation?

Mendel missed the comfort of operating at home. He was supposed to be fighting the Palestinians and the jihad in Hebron, not sitting on his ass in some American forest. He resisted the idea of leaving without Davisch. He could send another search party, but that would only delay the inevitable. If Davisch's men had encountered trouble, that meant the enemy was still out there.

Mendel couldn't compromise the mission. Loyalty went very far in the Kach-Kahane Chai brotherhood, but it never superseded duty. Sending Davisch out hadn't been the best decision. If he left his men behind, Ben-aryeh Pessach would be angry. It was possible he would strip Mendel of his rank and reduce him to a lowly servant.

There was a third possibility. Mendel could take just one man with him and go search for Davisch. It presented the least complication, and he could easily afford two hours. They were now ahead of schedule. According to the information provided to him, the American flight would hit the West Coast at 1100 hours. They would cross the Pacific and land in the Philippines to refuel. Then they would make the final stretch of their arduous journey to Israel.

Nobody would question the men. Two of the most powerful and influential nations in the world had already sanctioned the mission. That left little to stand in their way. The Kahane Chai would build the ACTEN device and use it to achieve their ends. Mendel hoped his superiors worked the device to its maximum potential. He wouldn't have presumed to tell them the best way to use it. Such things were beyond his grasp. He was a simple man fighting for a simple cause.

Mendel didn't trust Baram Herzhaft, but he trusted his own government even less. The political infrastructure in the entire Middle East was crumbling at best. It would be up to the Kach-Kahane movement to fuel the fire of revolution and the spirit of victory. They would take the reins from the weak and ineffectual, and they would topple their adversaries. They would grind them into dust.

The sound of the boat's engine roaring to life shook Mendel from his thoughts. He looked in the direction of the sound and stared hard at the canvas tent wall. He wanted to look through it, to see what the commotion was before he reacted to it. A moment passed before the sound of Galils and Uzis echoed in the morning air.

Mendel jumped from his seat and rushed outside.

THE EXECUTIONER GUNNED the engine and turned the wheel on the huge boat. The rear fans began to spin as he tried to swing the old craft around, but the creek bed was too shallow to allow for a turn. The soldier powered down and threw the engine selector into reverse. A choking sound rolled from the engine as it sputtered and died. The fans ground to a halt.

Bolan keyed the ignition and the engine fired again.

He slammed the selector into reverse, and the fans began to rotate. The boat started to move backward, and Bolan watched for obstructions, keeping himself centered on the waterway as his other eye marked the approaching terrorists.

Several of them reached the bank before the Executioner could create a sufficient distance. They dropped to their knees and began to open fire. Bolan brought his Uzi into play and aimed center mass on the closest target. He triggered a short burst, and the 9 mm rounds punched red holes in the man's stomach. The impact spun the terrorist away from the riverbank and deposited him roughly on the ground.

A second gunman began to rush toward the vessel as Bolan

finally gained enough water depth to complete a reverse turn. This time, he shifted into neutral and waited until the fans had slowed considerably. As the blades whirred to a halt, the soldier engaged the selector to a forward position and the fans obediently reversed direction. He quickly slammed the makeshift steering bar, and the boat started to rotate on its axis.

As the boat increased speed, Bolan turned his attention to the second terrorist sighting on his position.

The warrior unleashed a salvo of Uzi fire from the hip, sending up chunks of dirt at the man's feet. He threw himself to the deck of the boat as the terrorist returned fire with a Galil, apparently undaunted by the near hit. Autofire struck one of the fans, and sparks flew from the grille as the rounds pinged off the blades. It was enough to shatter the grille but not destroy the fan itself.

Bolan lined the Uzi sights on target and squeezed the trigger in two short bursts. The rounds struck their target, ripping flesh from the man's body. The terrorist fell forward as the weight from his upper torso lost its battle with gravity. He splashed facedown in the creek and lay still.

A tall man in desert fatigues emerged from the tent and shouted the hardforce into a pursuit. The Executioner smiled as he watched the terrorists rush for him.

His plan was working.

AS SOON AS YASSO SAW the Kahane Chai terrorists tear away to pursue Pollock, she knew it was time to make her move.

Only two guards remained at the rear of the plane, and there was no one left to load equipment. Movement from the tent caught her eye, and she struggled to make out the shadowy figure. A moment passed, and then the sunlight streaming through the thick stand of trees illuminated his face enough for her to make a positive identification.

Jurre Mendel! How many times had she stared at his picture and been briefed by her superiors at Mossad! This man was wanted for crimes she could barely utter, and there he was just thirty or forty meters away. He stood in a clearing, and it was as if he beckoned Yasso to wipe him from that existence.

She could take him from there.

She raised the Uzi and lined her sights on Mendel, but he dashed from view as she was triggering her weapon. The Uzi chattered and spit lead death at a target no longer present.

Yasso cursed herself as the guards saw the muzzle flashes, and returned fire. She rolled from her position and began to exchange bursts of 9 mm Parabellum rounds with the pair of Kahane terrorists. They tracked her movement, and as the rounds drew nearer she knew it was only a matter of time before they hit her with a lucky shot.

The Mossad agent couldn't help herself. Something was driving her to hunt Mendel like the animal she had come to know—and fear. The Kahane Chai leader was dangerous, and she couldn't let him escape. The ACTEN chips could wait. She realized her change in plans could compromise Pollock, and throw away their one opportunity to sabotage the plane. It didn't matter to her. She had watched the Kahane Chai murder innocent Americans, not to mention the innumerable bombings and assassinations they had masterminded against their own people.

Without Mendel, it was entirely possible they would accomplish the same thing. His leadership would be the only remaining factor holding the Kahane Chai together. If they saw Mendel was dead, they would probably consider the cause lost and abandon it.

Yasso performed a drastic move, stepping from the cover on the shore and jumping into the creek. The water rose to her thighs. The maneuver apparently surprised the two guards, and she gunned them down with well-aimed shots from the Uzi. They twisted and danced under the impact before falling to the ramp of the C-141.

Yasso turned her attention to Mendel's last position and realized the crucial error a moment too late. Mendel stood on the shore with a Jericho 941 pistol pointed directly at her head.

He smiled cruelly, and his dark eyes studied her with cool indifference.

"Put your weapon down, Mossad bitch," Mendel warned.

Yasso obeyed him, letting the Uzi splash into the creek.

"I no longer care what Herzhaft wants," he said. "I am going to kill you. But I am going to do it slowly."

BOLAN TOOK UP a new position to one side of the boat as he dropped an Uzi clip and slammed home a new one. He dropped the slide on the weapon and brought the muzzle into line with a tightly knit group of terrorists before they could get target acquisition.

The soldier fired a fresh burst of autofire. The 9 mm rounds drove some of the terrorists to seek cover as others dropped their comrades.

One gunman caught a Parabellum in the forehead. His weapon flew from his fingers as the force of the shot slammed him into a tree trunk.

A second terrorist doubled over as Bolan's fire mercilessly ripped through his legs and hips. The terrorist began to scream in agony as he dropped his weapon. Another quick pair of rounds permanently ended his pain.

The Executioner dropped a nearby terrorist who was about to toss a grenade. The spoon popped away as the bomb dropped next to the man and rolled into him. The resulting explosion rocked the shoreline and blew the terrorist's body into pieces. Chunks of bloody flesh and amputated limbs sailed in every direction, and doused the other terrorist gunmen nearby.

Bolan saw another pair of hardmen throw grenades simultaneously. One struck the front of the boat and bounced off, but the second struck the roof of the open-air cockpit and rolled onto the deck.

The soldier jumped off the vessel feetfirst before the grenade finished rolling. The first bomb blew beneath the water, churning a large wave and vibrating Bolan's feet.

A bright flash of light erupting on the boat immediately followed that explosion. Familiar white streams of light arched through the air. The Executioner realized that light had an all too familiar pattern even as it landed on the water surface around him and burst into white-hot sparks.

One speck struck his left arm.

The white phosphorous began to burn into his skin at the moment of contact. The soldier reached into the water and scooped a handful of mud from the bottom. He slapped the mud onto the wound as the smell of his own cooked flesh reached his nostrils. WP burned on oxygen; cutting the air supply would burn the incendiary and Bolan knew what he would have to do later.

The Executioner took up a firing position for maximum effect and sprayed the Kahane Chai gunners with a merciless hail of rounds. The two terrorists who had thrown the grenades fell first under the soldier's expert marksmanship. They toppled into each before collapsing into the creek.

Bolan fired another controlled burst at a trio of terrorists who had taken cover behind a small log. Splinters of wood hammered the terrorists as the soldier pinned them down with Uzi fire. He charged their position, continuing sustained bursts to keep them behind the log, reaching their hiding place just as his last clip died.

Bolan let the Uzi fall and drew his Desert Eagle as he stepped onto the log, blasting holes into the terrorists before they could bring their weapons to bear. Firing rifles on the warrior would have been futile given his proximity to them.

He holstered the Desert Eagle and unslung the Galil he'd placed on his back. He chambered the weapon and bent to strip the bodies of additional ammo clips for the Galil. He secured the spares and turned in the direction of the Kahane encampment.

Bolan had walked about ten paces when he detected the sounds of rushed movement in a brush line directly ahead. A new group of terrorists appeared, but they stopped short when they saw Bolan was ready for them.

The closest pair fell under a plethora of fiery rounds. The Galil barked continuously as the soldier depressed the trigger, the heavy rounds ripping through lung tissue and punching large, gaping holes out the backs of the terrorists.

The remaining three dived for cover, but Bolan tracked them with sustained bursts.

One of the terrorists managed to clear a side arm and snap-aimed at the warrior. Bolan jumped behind a tree to the right in time to avoid a double-tap of .45-caliber rounds. He whirled from the other side, now flanking the Kahane Chai gunman on the left. He fired a quick burst into the terrorist before the man could react. A corkscrew pattern drilled the terrorist's back at a cyclic rate of 550 rounds per minute. The 5.56 mm rounds tore through his spine with shearing force.

Bolan turned from the carnage and suddenly noted the boat had continued down the creek. The entire upper section was awash with flames. Hopefully, the vessel wouldn't catch the woods on fire. He didn't have the energy left to try to escape from a blazing forest.

There was no more resistance. The broken and bleeding bodies of at least a dozen terrorists lay scattered along the shore. He realized that his plan had succeeded. There was only one problem. It was a bit too quiet. A sudden pinch in his arm reminded him of the grisly task that now lay before him.

He leaned against a tree and drew his Colt Combat knife from its sheath. He then peeled the mud compress from the wound and clenched his teeth with agony as the oxygen struck the phosphorous and it began to burn again. Bolan shoved his knife into the skin and popped the slag from his arm, choking back his pain as he inspected the wound.

It was a wicked burn, deep enough to char the skin and leave a gray-white, leathery patch. There was no pain, which told the soldier it was a third-degree, full-thickness burn. He cut a piece of cloth from his fatigues and wrapped the injury.

The compress would at least keep out any dirt and debris until Bolan could have the wound treated properly. It would definitely add to the scars he'd collected over the years.

The Executioner pushed himself off the tree and continued for the enemy encampment. There would be very little resistance now. He could destroy the remaining opposition, and then he and Yasso could hike out of there and get back to civilization. Bolan was about ready for a long bout of R&R.

He continued toward the final showdown.

17

Aaron Kurtzman's plan worked.

The processor in his laptop hummed at full speed as it pulled and labeled files from the Fort Carson network with unerring accuracy. The chips were stacked against them as far as time was concerned, but the solution to the problem was simple.

All system files had a special extension. Kurtzman had written a program that could find and categorize these extensions, then sort them into appropriately labeled folders. Once that task was completed, it would simply be a matter of using the network backups to create a boot disk. This would bring the system online. From that point, he could reload the information and pray there was no physical damage to the hard drives.

Baram Herzhaft nodded at the screens with satisfaction. "It appears you are correct, Mr. Kershner. This might save us an inordinate amount of time."

"Thanks," Kurtzman replied dryly.

The Stony Man computer expert turned and looked at Herzhaft for a moment. The man didn't look good. Kurtzman wasn't sure if he was tired or ill, but the pale skin seemed obvious, even in the dim lighting. Herzhaft shook his head as he noted Kurtzman's concern, and his eyes pleaded with the man. Whatever was happening, he didn't want the others to know. Kurtzman decided to let it go.

"How long will it take?" Brognola asked him.

Brognola, Dunham and Wasserman had arrived a few

minutes earlier. The rest of the base was anxiously awaiting the revival of their systems. Technicians were posted at every computer station attached to the network. The anticipation was almost too much to bear, but Kurtzman wasn't about to let that break his concentration.

He would need every faculty to overcome the problem at hand.

"It's hard to say." Kurtzman shook his head and shrugged as he studied the computer terminal. "It depends on how large each of the system files are, and basically how fast my computer can process them."

"There's no way to speed things up some?" Brognola queried.

Kurtzman brightened as a new idea came to him. "I just thought of something. We could link up with the hardware at the Farm."

He reached down to his belt and withdrew the cellular phone clipped there. He punched a number on the keypad and it automatically dialed the phone. After two rings, the scrambler kicked in. It would prevent any electronic device from intercepting the transmission.

Price answered. "Hey, guy. What's up?"

"I need to do a link with my laptop and the mainframe there. I'm coding the modem signals, and I want you to key the computer to unscramble the information and sort the files as they come through. As the files become available, you can send them back through the line as attachments. Got it?"

"I think so," Price acknowledged with some trepidation in her voice.

"Just follow my instructions and everything will be okay."

"Check." She paused and then added, "Has there been any word from him?"

"Not yet, but we're working on that angle, as well." Kurtzman spared a glance at Brognola to indicate Price had asked about Bolan.

"Okay," Price replied. "Good luck, Aaron."

Kurtzman waited until he heard the modem tones, then hooked the cellular phone into an interface on the back of his laptop. There was about a ten-second delay, and suddenly the files began to flash on his screen at an unfathomable rate.

Kurtzman grinned and tossed Brognola a victorious look. "It's working."

"Good job," Brognola said.

He turned to look at Wasserman with a confident expression. There was no question the post commander had his doubts about their ability to overcome the problem. The U.S. Army wasn't used to outsiders showing them up, and this was one more notch on Stony Man's belt. The general could leave Kurtzman to his own devices and turn his attention to other matters.

"I would imagine we can have your tactical systems up within the hour at the rate we're going," Brognola told Wasserman. "I'd like to set a plan in motion that will facilitate a rescue operation as quickly as possible."

"What kind of rescue?" Wasserman asked.

"I don't have time to get into that now. I'm going to have to ask you to trust me on this issue. I'll be happy to explain it later, but right now I need to secure those chips and find one of our men. He may be in trouble."

"You're talking about our agreement," Wasserman stated.

"Yes."

"Very well, sir." Wasserman turned to Dunham. "Major, I'll stay here with these two gentleman in case they need any further resources. You may take Mr. Brognola wherever he wants to go, and provide him with whatever he asks for. However, nothing leaves until you have my personal clearance. Understood?"

"Yes, sir," Dunham replied with a salute.

Wasserman returned it. "Carry on."

Dunham gestured for Brognola to step outside, and he followed him downstairs to the motor pool. They climbed into

Wasserman's Hummer and Brognola indicated he wished to go to the airfield.

The first item on the agenda would be to retrieve Grimaldi. They wouldn't need to leave Fort Carson any time soon, so the pilot would be of more use leading the search party for Bolan.

"Will you need aircraft for this mission, sir?" Dunham asked.

"Absolutely," Brognola said. "At least two gunships, and possibly a third. I'll also need about a dozen of your best troops."

"Done," Dunham replied. "Where do you plan to send them, sir?"

"That's a tough one. I have information that leads me to believe the people responsible for compromising your security are operating in a region just southwest of here. Are you familiar with a place called Royal Gorge Park?"

"Yes, sir," Dunham admitted with a shrug. "It's a tourist attraction. Do you think that's where these people are hiding?"

"I'd be willing to stake my life on it," Brognola replied grimly.

THERE WAS NO QUESTION that Mack Bolan was in serious trouble.

Barbara Price had pulled out all the stops with her intelligence connections at the Mossad. She'd gleaned any information she could on the ACTEN device, and probed every avenue to determine who else would benefit from its abilities.

The fact they now had Herzhaft in their possession was an embarrassment Mossad couldn't afford without further straining relations between two friendly nations. While she might have overstepped her bounds, Price wasn't concerned. Brognola would understand her need to establish solid leads on Bolan's current status.

The current status was ugly.

Mossad believed their agent, Ilia Yasso, might be working in concert with Herzhaft. On the other hand, it was possible Yasso didn't have a clue Herzhaft had sold out to the Kahane Chai. In either case, if she was alive and Bolan was with her, they wouldn't have the knowledge Price had.

At that moment, Israel Defense Forces troops were mounting a major strike against an operation in the desert southeast of Jerusalem. With the assistance of state-of-the-art satellite photography, Stony Man had pinpointed the possible headquarters of a Kach-Kahane Chai base. Price had no qualms about leaking this information to the Mossad counterterrorist section. If the Kahane Chai was operating in that area, it was in for a rude surprise. In return, Mossad cooperated extensively with information about Yasso and the entire operation.

There was another complication—one of which Bolan might not be aware. The Kahane Chai hardmen apparently weren't the only major players in this game of cat-and-mouse. FBI records indicated one of the men found near Royal Gorge Park was a Hamas terrorist.

Price's heart ached for the warrior, but she wouldn't have admitted it.

She couldn't admit it.

More often than not, it was difficult to remain neutral in such situations. She couldn't remember the last time she'd seen Bolan as tired as he appeared at the airport. He was exhausted and deservedly so—his war against terrorism and oppression was a never-ending one.

The Executioner's arm's-length alliance with his government leaked into his relationship with Price. She'd never dreamed of marriage; it wouldn't have worked out because of their individual capacities. Bolan was a loner and he would always be that way. He was the consummate warrior who followed his own path. He did things on his terms because they worked.

Price never pressured him for more than what he was willing to give. Bolan wasn't that kind of man. Besides, the hurt and betrayal she'd felt after her divorce with Kevin Shawnessy had left walls. Mack Bolan had broken through some of those walls. He'd restored her faith in men, and established a new goal for her. Their moments together at the Farm were stolen passion, sure, but they were a little more than that to her.

The Executioner had a way of instilling confidence in every spirit he touched. She owed him—they all owed him. An ungrateful and unforgiving country owed him, even while it turned its head in complacency or condemned the man for his methods.

Well, she didn't condemn him. She would never condemn him.

A control panel beeped for her attention. Price rolled her chair to the keyboard and began to return the files to Kurtzman. He had cleverly rigged the system to automatically exchange information. The computers hummed and whirred with blinding speed, and the din increased in the operations center.

Millions of bytes of information were transferred per second. Stony Man boasted a retrieval and transmission network that was second to none. The government had spared no expense to provide them with the most sophisticated computer system in the world. In comparison to Kurtzman, Price was a hack. Nevertheless, she possessed the genius necessary to operate smoothly and efficiently.

Her fingers flew over the keyboard, and the computer responded immediately to her commands. The information exchange continued, and Price never wavered. The tension was mounting. She could only hope they were able to restore the systems at Fort Carson in time.

Bolan was counting on her.

There was no way in hell she would let the big guy down.

JACK GRIMALDI GRINNED at Brognola as they disembarked from the jet.

"If there's any way at all I can help him, count me in, Hal."

"I already have," Brognola replied.

The two men climbed into the Hummer where Dunham waited, and soon they were bound for the chopper hangar on the other side of the post.

Grimaldi wanted to ask a million questions but he held himself in check. It was neither the time nor the place for a Q&A session. He'd have plenty of time to sort it all out later. For the moment, there were more pressing matters.

Brognola didn't have to elaborate anyway. The mission would probably be simple enough. Grimaldi's expertise as a pilot would likely be tested to the limits this time. He couldn't count the number of times he'd had to pull the Executioner out of one harrowing situation or another. Their relationship was founded on mutual trust and respect.

Actually, Grimaldi was proud of his position with the Stony Man organization. He had the reputation of being a miracle worker. He'd built that reputation by coming through at the last moment. When the chips were down, Grimaldi answered the call for help.

Mack Bolan had seen something in Grimaldi that the pilot hadn't seen in himself. It was the fundamental key to their friendship. Grimaldi had spent his early days flying for the Mafia because he hadn't felt he was worth more than that. The Executioner renewed that spirit of self-worth, and Grimaldi would always be grateful—and there it was.

It was time to go to work.

KURTZMAN WATCHED with excitement as the file attachments began to reappear. They were no longer fragments, but complete and viable files. He began to sort them into their respective places. The terminal lit up, and the CPU in a stand to his left began to click and buzz with new life.

"Okay!" Kurtzman exclaimed. He slapped his hands together and rubbed them with delight. "Now we're in business!"

Price had pulled it off, and she deserved as much credit as

anyone did. Kurtzman couldn't shake the sense that something in her voice was hesitant. Hell, it was more like fear. Operating the system on that end was important, but it was hardly an insurmountable task. He couldn't believe she would have balked at the task.

The two were close, and Kurtzman was a bit angry he hadn't realized something was wrong until after the fact. It wasn't just concern for the fate of Mack Bolan. There was something she'd discovered, something that changed the circumstances. It was too late now, so there was no point in worrying about it. He had to focus on his present mission. Price could take care of herself.

The .bat files finished loading, and Kurtzman began to hammer at the keyboard. His sharp mind focused on every character. He had the initiation program from his own system memorized. It was risky keying the information in binary format, but it was the simplest method and the computer could always read the universal format of ones and zeros.

A few minutes passed and suddenly the generators buried deep in basement of the building rumbled. Lights flickered at first, and then they blinked on and continued to burn brightly. The jangle of a telephone from somewhere nearby startled Kurtzman, but he pushed it from his mind and began to work through the system.

"Post headquarters, General Wasserman's office, this is an unsecured line. May I help you?" Lieutenant Cynthia Asher's voice announced. "Yes, we know it's working! Stand by your stations and wait for further instructions."

General Wasserman leaped from his chair and rushed to clap Kurtzman on the shoulder.

"Kershner, I don't know who you are or where you came from, but I'm going to tell Brognola to put you in for the Medal of Honor."

"Yes, sir," Kurtzman replied with glee.

Wasserman moved back to his desk and lifted the receiver. "Sergeant?" Wasserman barked. "This is General Wasserman. Get me the company commander at Charlie, Third Brigade, and pronto.'' A moment of silence elapsed before the call was transferred. "Captain Haddow? Your unit is under immediate emergency deployment. In a few minutes, Major Dunham will be arriving with a man from Washington. You are to give him whatever cooperation he asks for and no questions asked. Understood? Out here.''

Wasserman slammed down the phone and walked to his door.

"Lieutenant Asher?"

"Yes, sir?"

"Get the CO at MAST headquarters on the phone and tell him I want his unit up and ready in twenty minutes! I want every pilot, every door gunner and every flight crew on standby and all of their backups, as well."

"Yes, sir!"

Wasserman looked at Herzhaft and smiled, but the old man's face had gone pale.

"Are you all right, sir?" Wasserman asked. He crossed the room and reached for the man, but Herzhaft couldn't seem to reply.

Kurtzman turned his attention toward the Mossad scientist and realized there was big trouble. Herzhaft was as white as a sheet, and sweat had broken out on his forehead. He suddenly clutched a hand to his chest, and his breathing started coming in wheezing gasps. He moved his lips, but he couldn't produce a sound other than gurgling squeals.

"Oh, my God," Kurtzman said, "he's having a heart attack. Call an ambulance. Now!"

MAJOR DUNHAM LEANED on the Hummer's brakes and brought the vehicle to a grinding halt in front of the building that housed the Third BCT's headquarters.

The trio piled from the vehicle with Dunham in the lead. Two MPs saluted the post XO as he passed them. He ignored the gesture and shot them a simple nod. His mind was racing on the sudden turn of events. They had done it! Whoever these men were, they had done what a dozen experts couldn't. They deserved every bit of credit, and Dunham had found a new admiration for Brognola and his team.

A lithe man in BDUs and full combat gear saluted Dunham, and this time he returned it.

"First Sergeant Walsh?"

"Yes, sir!"

"Are your men ready?"

"Yes, sir."

Dunham turned and gestured to Brognola and Grimaldi.

"These men are acting under the authority of myself and General Wasserman. They have a mission for you, and I want nothing but the best."

"We're ready, sir," Walsh snapped.

"Fine. I need two teams of light infantry soldiers with rifles and ammunition. While I can't go into the details, we have possible foreign enemy troops on American soil. They will be well equipped and well armed, so get the best you have and transport them out to your parade field. We'll pick them up in choppers shortly."

"Yes, sir!"

Brognola sighed with satisfaction. Hang in there, Striker.

18

There were less than a dozen Kahane Chai troops remaining.

This thought left the Executioner with mixed feelings of doubt and suspicion as he studied the encampment while concealed behind tall brush. There was no movement near the C-141, and the hum of the generators was absent. The only sounds the soldier could detect were the babble of the creek, the call of birds and the buzzing of insects.

The camp looked deserted.

Yasso's mission had been to take out the remaining resistance from cover, then disable the plane with the M-203. In the absence of bodies, Bolan had to assume she'd failed in that mission. Was she dead or had she used the diversion to make her own insidious move? It was possible she'd been waiting for such an opportunity.

He would find out soon enough.

Bolan couldn't dispel the sense the Kahane Chai was lying in wait for him. The entire business smelled of a trap. He wasn't about to go rushing blindly into it to the satisfaction of his enemy. It was time to outwit them—beat them at their own game. The big guy formulated a quick plan and crawled backward into the woods.

He withdrew about fifty yards, then began to encircle the camp. The terrorists would be expecting him to return from that direction. Whoever was in charge would probably stagger the terrorists along the wood line with instructions to wait until a target presented itself.

Bolan wouldn't have dreamed of disappointing the opposition.

The warrior continued through the thick forestry. He used the shadows and cover to gain the advantage of assault on the rear flank. When the moment came, he would unleash a hail of destruction the Kahane Chai wouldn't soon forget. He would do it for Jacoby, and all of the good men who had died at the hands of the terror group.

And he would do it because it was his duty.

YASSO WATCHED Jurre Mendel from her position inside the tent.

She tugged at the heavy rope that bound her to a cot, the coarse fibers rubbing her wrists raw. Despite the rope burns, the movement felt good. The terrorist leader had tied her hands tightly, and at least her struggles allowed some circulation to return to her palms and fingers.

Mendel turned from where he was stacking the last remnants of any papers that could trace the operation to the Kahane Chai. He studied her with resolute anger as she continued to fight her bonds. An amused smile crossed his lips. That only served to strengthen Yasso's resolve, and she couldn't quench the hatred she felt for him.

"You might as well kill me, Mendel," she spit. "Because if I get free, I will strangle you with my bare hands."

"Shut up," Mendel warned calmly. "You will do nothing. I must return you to Israel to guarantee Baram Herzhaft's cooperation. Beyond that, I will torment you for days before I allow you the sweet mercy of death."

"What?" Yasso asked with disbelief. "What does Herzhaft have to do with this?"

"Oh, he didn't tell you?" Mendel asked with mock innocence. "That is too bad. He sold you out, woman. Just like he sold out the Mossad."

"I don't believe it."

"Yes, you do. You just do not want to admit it. How else

do you think we would have been able to steal the ACTEN chips?''

''I don't know what you're talking about.''

Mendel smiled another one of his cruel smiles, and Yasso would have pulled his face off if she were free.

''You seem to forget that Herzhaft is as tired of the Israeli cabinet's pathetic response to the Arab threat as my own superior officers.'' He sat at his desk and crossed his legs. ''You know it is true, what I have told you. Woman, you are my one last tool of barter. Herzhaft is enamored with you, although I cannot imagine why.''

''You are wrong, Mendel,'' Yasso replied. ''Just as wrong as that delusional Yusef Nahum. You will die just as he did.''

''I suppose you are going to tell me that it was you who killed him?''

''No,'' she said. ''He died at the hands of the man who has destroyed your plans from the very beginning. And you will die by his hands in the same manner.''

''Hardly,'' Mendel snorted. ''This man you speak of, what is his name?''

''I know him as Colonel Pollock. He fights like a professional soldier. He has single-handedly wiped out your force. You will never bring him down, Mendel. Never. He will hunt you and kill you in your sleep. I no longer care what you do to me, because I know he will destroy you and your filthy regime.''

''We shall see. However, I am very curious to know why you do not share the Kach-Kahane Chai's views. As I recall, someone very important to you fell victim to those we abhor.''

Yasso stared at Mendel for a moment. ''How did you know that?''

''We keep track of every such cowardly act. Despite what you might believe, Mossad woman, we consider all Jewish life to be sacred.''

''The only thing sacred to you is the leader of your organization and his twisted doctrine. He has perverted the aims of our government and twisted them to suit his own ends."

"On the contrary. We are angered when our own fall. What we do is for the good of our country and our people. Herzhaft realizes this and that is why he agreed to help us retrieve this American technology."

"You mean steal."

"If you like," Mendel said, inclining his head. "We could use someone of your talents, but you obviously do not understand the importance of our mission. Therefore, if you are not for us then we must assume you are against us."

"You are a sick man."

"Perhaps."

The distant sound of the C-141's engines droned in their ears.

"It is time to go," Mendel snapped.

He rose from his chair, untied Yasso from the cot and roughly hauled her to her feet. She tried to kick him, but he used the sole of his boot to deflect the blow. He yanked on her ropes, hauled her in front of him and brutally shoved her toward the entrance.

Yasso suddenly felt the point of a knife at her spine, and she stiffened.

"Do not resist me, woman," Mendel whispered in her ear. "You are more valuable to me alive than dead, but I will not hesitate to kill you. Remember that."

THE EXECUTIONER SPOTTED a Kahane terrorist standing near the plane as he reached the north side of the camp. The rear of the aircraft was now facing him, and Bolan estimated the target was about seventy yards away. He was raising his Galil to take out the guard when the engines of the C-141 roared to life.

Time was up!

Bolan's eyes moved in the direction of the tent and a moment passed before Yasso appeared. The man who followed her out carried himself with the authority and confidence of a hardened leader. As they walked toward the plane, the soldier could see Yasso's hands were tied behind her, and the nameless terrorist held something to the small of her back. He couldn't discern what it was, but then it didn't really matter.

Somehow, the Kahane had managed to capture her.

Bolan didn't hear the terrorist who crept up behind him. The man launched himself against the soldier and knocked him prone to the ground. The assailant tried to get his arm around Bolan's neck, but the Executioner didn't plan to give him that quarter. He was still functioning on a mixture of adrenaline and determination, and the terrorist had picked the wrong man to jump.

The Executioner twisted onto his side drove an elbow into his assailant's temple, following up with a second blow to the jaw. A loud pop signaled a dislocation, and the Kahane Chai killer rolled off. Bolan brought the Galil into play and slammed the end of the stock into his enemy's face. His skull caved in, and the man choked on his own blood.

Bolan regained his feet and turned the muzzle of the Galil in the direction of the first terrorist he'd spotted. He triggered a burst, the 5.56 mm rounds landing in a tight shot pattern and nearly ripping the surprised gunman in two. Blood and intestines spilled from the terrorist's gut as he flopped onto his back.

The soldier saw that Yasso and her captor had stopped. The terrorist looked in his direction, and for a moment the Executioner could have sworn the man was smiling. He turned and pushed Yasso in the direction of the rear cargo door.

Bolan took a couple of steps toward the plane and aimed his weapon at one of the jet props. The movement of men behind him screamed for his attention. A wave of Kahane terrorists appeared from the east side of the wood line and rushed his position.

Bolan crouched as he whirled, raising the Galil to his shoulder. He began to shoot the enemy troops with controlled, accurate bursts.

One of the terrorists tripped over his comrade, who was the first to die under the Executioner's marksmanship. The man rolled out of the fall, got to his feet and leveled his weapon in Bolan's direction. The big man saw the threat and quickly dealt with it. Two rounds drilled through the terrorist's chest, and he dropped to his knees as his finger curled reflexively around the trigger.

The rounds from his weapon spit harmlessly into the sky.

STATIC FILTERED over the speaker of the radio aboard the Sikorsky CH-3.

"MAST zero-seven-niner from flight control, you are cleared for takeoff."

Affectionately known as the Jolly Green Giant, the CH-3 required a crew of two. Jack Grimaldi powered up the engines and cast one more look in Brognola's direction. The Stony Man chief tossed him a two-finger salute, and Grimaldi gave him a thumbs-up before grabbing the stick.

The powerful transport lifted off smoothly and the craft immediately responded to his deft handle of its controls.

That particular CH-3 was one of several assigned to Fort Carson's military air search and rescue team. Two turboshaft engines on top of the body midsection powered the sleek chopper. The CH-3 carried only miniguns since its primary purpose was the transport of troops for assault, search, and rescue missions. It had a capacity for thirty equipped soldiers. The present company numbered about half that.

Grimaldi checked his six to insure the escorts were following. A pair of Hughes AH-64 Apache gunships followed at a safe distance. They were a familiar sight to the ace pilot, but no less a comforting one. Their armament included a 30 mm chain gun, Hellfire missiles and HE rockets. They were some of the most fearsome attack helicopters in the U.S. Army arsenal, and Grimaldi had flown his share.

The Stony Man pilot double-checked the coordinates and

increased the CH-3's thrust and attitude controls. The trip to Royal Gorge Park would take less than twenty minutes.

Grimaldi could only hope they would be in time.

BOLAN JUMPED to his feet and raced for cover behind a tree as rounds chewed up the earth around him. On his run, he dropped the magazine from the Galil and replaced it. The soldier reached the tree and found cover in time to avoid a hail of lead.

He knelt quickly and swung the muzzle of his weapon around the edge of the tree. Some of the terrorists dived to the ground, but a few couldn't escape Bolan's fury. The cover allowed him the advantage. Several troops fell under the soldier's merciless gunfire. The Galil smoked under the punishment and the bolt clacked back and forth with each round fired.

The terrorists brave enough to charge his position toppled one upon another as the heavy-caliber slugs tore through their bellies, chests and heads.

Several terrorists who had dropped to the ground attempted to rise and execute a flanking action against their enemy. Bolan dropped them with a fresh hail of autofire. During a lull in the combat, he dropped another clip and replaced it. He was down to two clips, and his only other option was the Desert Eagle.

He would fight bare-handed if he had to, but it was going to end here one way or another.

A massive explosion suddenly erupted from the tent, and pieces of flaming canvas flew through the air. Another explosion followed it, this one placed almost in the dead center of the camp, and tons of dirt and rock were scattered across the battlefield. More explosions ensued along the perimeter, headed straight toward Bolan.

The remaining terrorists died under the combined forces of superheated gases and concussion. The explosions tore through their fragile bodies like flames through rice paper, ripping off their limbs and hurling their bodies through the hazy air.

The Executioner realized the cause. The Kahane had rigged

the place with explosives, and they were set for timed detonation. They meant to destroy valuable evidence and cover an escape.

Bolan was on his feet and moving as the cacophony of blasts assailed his ears. He rushed into the clearing and sprinted for the cargo plane. The ramp began to retract as the plane started to roll down the makeshift runway. Whoever held Yasso captive had planned his escape well. Bolan pushed himself to the limits of physical endurance, sucking vital oxygen into his lungs.

His heart pounded against his chest and his ears rang from the powder keg that had almost blown him to bits. He reached the airstrip, forcing his mind into a single purpose. Despite his efforts, he couldn't match the pace of the four powerful engines that propelled the C-141. He slowed to a trot and watched helplessly as the wheels left the ground.

Bolan raised the Galil and emptied the clip but to no avail.

His enemy had escaped.

THE ROYAL GORGE BRIDGE hung below the trio of Army helicopters now circling the park. There were no tourists present, only a few police squads and some plainclothes with unmarked units.

Grimaldi's hopes sank.

He could see some other vehicles lined up near the entrance to the park—shiny black vans that appeared to fulfill only one purpose. The transport of bodies. Grimaldi prayed the Executioner wasn't among the dead. Something in his gut told him the big guy was alive. He had to be.

The copilot tapped Grimaldi on the shoulder and pointed to a large column of dark smoke to the southwest. It was barely visible given the distance, but it was there. A renewed hope sprang into Grimaldi's consciousness and he maneuvered the Sikorsky in that direction. There was no guarantee it was anything other than a forest fire, but Grimaldi was going to check it out anyway.

He turned the selector switch on his communications unit and addressed the pilots in the Apaches.

"Attention, Foxtrot-Echo three and four, this MAST zero-seven-niner. I have smoke sighted at about two-twenty-nine, estimate twelve miles. Follow my lead."

He cut off the device and opened the throttle. The powerful engines whined in protest, but Grimaldi pushed the craft onward. He knew its limits. They weren't carrying a tremendous load, and the Army knew how to maintain its aircraft.

As they drew closer, Grimaldi let the Sikorsky dip until he was only twenty or thirty yards above the tree line. With the heavy woods of the San Isabel Forest stretching below him, he couldn't imagine the difficult task of searching for a lone figure.

Another thought crossed the pilot's mind and it caused him to smile. Brognola had mentioned a rescue operation. That would mean they were searching for the lost. If anything, the Executioner might be alone but he would never be lost. They had a better chance of getting lost than the big guy did. If he knew Bolan at all, he was probably right where he wanted to be, and there was a good chance he was kicking ass to boot.

They were about a mile from the smoke when the large shadow of a C-141 burst from the cover of trees and climbed into the sky. Grimaldi was startled to see the massive bird emerge from such a small clearing. The markings indicated U.S. Army, but Grimaldi was guessing there was more to the story.

He flipped on the all-system and keyed his mike again. "Foxtrot-Echo three and four, cargo plane spotted at two-eight-one. Pursue and observe, but do not engage until further orders."

The respective pilots in the Apaches signaled their compliance as Grimaldi took the Sikorsky into a steep descent. They hit the clearing, and he immediately spotted the familiar form of a man waving his arms at them. Grimaldi wouldn't have believed it if he hadn't seen it with his own eyes. He applied braking thrust and spun the sleek CH-3 into a tight turn.

The main rotor increased speed as Grimaldi set the Sikorsky

on the makeshift airstrip in a perfect landing. The blades churned dust and debris, and Mack Bolan emerged through the haze.

Grimaldi ordered the copilot to keep the massive helicopter under control before jumping from his seat and pushing his way into the rear. As he moved toward the side door with unchecked fervor, he could sense the presence of the Executioner close to him. It was almost as if the two shared some kind of spirit.

The Stony Man pilot yanked the door aside and grinned when he found Bolan staring back at him. The soldier looked tired and beat-up, but there was something in those cold blue eyes that signaled the job wasn't over yet. Despite some visible injuries, his friend didn't look too bad for the hardships he'd obviously endured in the past twenty-four hours.

"Hey, Sarge!" Grimaldi hollered over the whirling blades and whining engines. "Need a lift?"

"You know it," Bolan replied. He stepped inside and closed the door behind him.

The two men shook hands, and Grimaldi could sense the relief that spread across the soldier's face. He was glad to see Bolan was alive, no matter what his condition.

"You saw the plane?" Bolan asked sharply.

"Yeah, I've got two Apaches on it. I take it there aren't friendlies aboard?"

"One," Bolan replied grimly. "I wish I could say there wasn't, because then we could just blow it out of the sky."

A fresh grin cracked Grimaldi's face. "Well, let's see if we can bring her down in one piece."

"Yeah."

Bolan dropped to one knee and tried to ignore the surprised looks on the dozen-plus faces of infantry soldiers that stared at him. The Executioner had no idea how Grimaldi managed to find him, but he didn't really care at that point. The only important thing now was to bring that plane down, and finish the mission. And this time, there was no escape.

19

IV lines dripped precious fluids into Baram Herzhaft's body.

Brognola watched the Mossad scientist with mixed feelings. The soft breathing, sickly color and failure to regain consciousness all pointed to less than fifty-fifty odds of recovery. According to the post physician, Herzhaft apparently had suffered a previous heart attack, which the doctor suspected had gone untreated.

Brognola considered the situation.

A C-141 was currently under surveillance, and Grimaldi had reported that Striker was okay. This was a relief, considering the odds the warrior had faced. He took a deep breath and could hardly contain the pride he felt. To be associated with a man like Mack Bolan wasn't a matter of pride really. It was a matter of honor—*his* honor.

Since the first day Brognola had approached Bolan with amnesty, and met the soldier face-to-face, he knew there wasn't another man quite like him.

The Executioner fought the battles nobody else wanted to, save for the members of Phoenix Force and Able Team. He was hard right down to the bone, but he had a heart as large as the life itself. He cared about his country and he cared about the innocent. Many would have perished aeons ago had it not been for the courage and determination of one man.

Herzhaft let out a soft moan and his eyes slowly opened.

Brognola leaned forward in his chair and stared at the man. He could almost sense the imminent death, and he needed to get some answers. The Army doctors had ordered rest, but Brognola didn't give a damn. If there was something else they needed to know, something they had missed, the time to get the information was now.

Because there probably wasn't going to be a later.

"Dr. Herzhaft?" Brognola addressed him quietly.

Herzhaft turned and appeared to focus his eyes on Brognola. He was on pain medication, and an anticoagulant to keep any further clots from developing in the coronary arteries. The damage to his heart was extensive, and unless he recovered sufficiently from this latest attack, the chances of bypass surgery increasing his survival were negligible.

"Dr. Herzhaft?" Brognola repeated. "I need to talk to you."

"I...am...listening," Herzhaft said with a weak smile.

"We're still trying to restore all of the systems to the post. Is there anything else we need to know about this procedure? Anything that you might have forgotten or failed to disclose?"

"N-no. Kershn—" He took a ragged breath and started again. "Everything is on...the disk. Kershner has everything...he needs to finish the job. He is a smart man, a...a good man."

"Yes, he is," Brognola agreed.

Herzhaft reached out and grabbed Brognola's hand.

The move made the Stony Man chief feel a bit awkward, but he didn't draw away. Despite Herzhaft's crimes against Israel and America, he was still dying. Brognola could see no reason to deny the man a little comfort and peace in his last moments in this life.

"Tell...tell Ilia," Herzhaft said, straining to be heard, "that...I am sorry for betraying her. Tell her I love her. Tell her—"

The breath left him and he died quietly. The monitors began to beep as his heart and breathing ceased.

The Army medical staff rushed into the room and prepared to begin resuscitation, but Brognola stopped them.

"Let him go," he said quietly.

As THE C-141 CONTINUED to gain altitude, the Hughes AH-64 Apaches flitted around it. The gunners were ready, their weapons armed and missiles locked. They were itching for a fight, though the unarmed C-141 was no match for a pair of attack choppers.

Bolan watched the show through the front windscreen from his position just aft of the cockpit seats as Grimaldi lifted off the ground and opened the engines wide on the CH-3. They rushed toward the action, and the Executioner could feel his stomach leap into his throat as the ace Stony Man pilot maneuvered the Sikorsky.

The soldier lifted one of the headsets hanging on a hook and donned it.

"We need to bring it down easy, Jack. No more and no less. I'll take care of the rest."

"Roger, Sarge," Grimaldi replied. He flipped the radio switch to the open frequency. "Foxtrot-Echo three and four from MAST zero-seven-niner. Target the starboard engines and open fire. Repeat, target engines on the starboard side and fire at will."

Lances of light arced from the 30 mm chain guns as heavy-caliber tracer rounds hammered the C-141. The first engine erupted into flame, scorching the wing, and moments later it dissipated as the pilot cut off the engine. They knocked the second engine out of commission in a similar fashion. Clouds of dark smoke began to pour from the crippled plane, and it immediately lost climbing angle.

The nose began to drop, and the starboard wing rose with the change in power. The best the plane could do now was circle without starboard engines to support and balance the craft. Bolan knew it wasn't heavily loaded, which meant the pilots had a fighting chance to bring the huge cargo plane down safely. It was putting civilians below at risk, but there were no remaining options. They couldn't allow the Kahane Chai to escape with the ACTEN technology.

The plane began to dip and buck under the buffeting mountain winds. The Executioner knew it was only a matter of time before they decided bringing her down was an acceptable alternative to nursing the craft out of American airspace.

As if the pilots had read the soldier's thoughts, the plane began to descend.

MENDEL LEFT YASSO TIED to a handhold in the main cargo hold and navigated his way to the cockpit.

"What is going on?" he demanded.

"American Army gunships, sir," the copilot replied through clenched teeth.

The C-141 began to buck and shake as the two men fought to keep altitude and the nose level.

"They took out two engines on one side," the pilot explained. "We can't fly without at least one of them functional. We have to land."

Mendel whipped the Jericho pistol from his holster and pointed it at the pilot's head. The copilot looked at Mendel with surprise, but neither of the men would have tried to overpower him. Mendel stared at them, his breath hot and his eyes burning with a fanatical glow.

"Under no circumstances are you to bring this plane down. You go as far as you can."

"S-sir," the copilot stammered, "we have gone as far as we can. If we don't land now, we will crash and be destroyed."

"My soul is prepared," Mendel said viciously. "If that is our destiny, then so be it."

He turned, left the cockpit and went back to where he'd left Yasso. She smiled at him in the same cruel way he'd done so many times with her. He knew there was no escape, and he was certain she realized it. He sensed the tide was turning against him—just as Yasso had predicted—and he was becoming increasingly unstable. Sooner or later, he would make a mistake, and she would attempt to take advantage of that.

"It appears you have failed after all, Jurre," Yasso announced triumphantly.

"Perhaps," Mendel agreed. "However, at least I will enjoy the pleasure of watching you crash and burn with this plane."

The C-141 dipped toward the ground, and Mendel knew it was no use to threaten the pilots further. It was in the hands of God now. He found a jump seat and lifted the seat cushion. The unmistakable square pack of a parachute was secured there. He reached down, unbuckled the straps and lifted the pack from its hiding spot.

Mendel expertly stepped into the harness. If the big American was going to pursue him, he would have to sprout wings and fly to do it. As a veteran soldier in the Kahane Chai brotherhood, Mendel had learned that the most successful warrior was one who would do the unpredictable at the most unexpected moment. It was all about decisive action, something to which the terrorist was no stranger.

He couldn't contain some feelings of anger. Pollock had interfered with the operation from the beginning. Mendel had seen him fighting back at the operations site. It seemed that some energy or power walked with the man, as if a ghostly hand of protection were wrapped around him. He was almost a wraith—perhaps a demon in a man's body.

Mendel walked to the rear of the plane and hooked his parachute to the static line overhead. He flipped the cargo-door release and watched the ramp begin to fall obediently. The plane shifted and nearly tossed Mendel out of the back before he was ready. He latched on to a handhold and waited until the ramp was sufficiently extended before releasing his hold.

With a quick salute to Yasso, he ran across the ramp and jumped into free air. Four seconds elapsed before the chute opened and yanked him roughly against the harness. As he began to drop toward the mountainous region below, he smiled.

He had escaped the foolish Americans. One day, he would return.

GRIMALDI POINTED at the small figure that leaped from the C-141.

"Look, Sarge!"

"I see it," Bolan replied easily. He turned to the copilot. "You got any chutes aboard this bird?"

The copilot nodded and jerked his thumb to indicate they were in the rear stowage area.

Bolan put a firm hand on Grimaldi's shoulder. "Stick with the plane, Jack. I'm going after our jumper."

"You got it."

The Executioner removed his headset and rushed to the rear of the helicopter. The same group of eyes that had first stared at him when he'd boarded now watched with interest. He searched the rear storage compartments and quickly located a chute. He donned the harness as he nodded in the direction of the door and ordered one of the soldiers to open it.

At first, the infantryman looked at him with surprise. A quick scowl was enough to change the trooper's mind, and he immediately rose and unlatched the door.

When Bolan was in position, he tossed a quick nod at the reluctant man. The door slid aside and the warrior was out in a flash. He was in a rather sticky situation. He was maybe six or seven thousand feet high, but he would have to do a considerable free fall to come down in proximity to the target.

Bolan didn't have to guess who his mystery quarry might be. It was obviously the Kahane Chai leader he'd spotted with Yasso. Only one person had left the C-141, which meant the Mossad agent was still aboard the cargo plane. The terrorist had probably killed her already, which gave tracking and eliminating the lone enemy double purpose.

The rush of air at that elevation felt good against the sweat that soaked the soldier's body. He quickly spotted the terrorist leader's parachute and judged the attitude and direction. Bolan curled into a ball and somersaulted until he achieved a headlong dive.

The wind was with him and pushed his body toward the target.

He continued his fall until he reached about fifteen hundred feet. He twisted again and as his body reached the critical point, he yanked the rip cord. The parachute deployed at roughly a thousand feet. Bolan grabbed the risers and steered himself into position. He assessed the surrounding terrain, then focused his energies on the landing.

The enemy's chute had disappeared in the trees, but the Executioner already knew the location of the drop point. He maneuvered himself with alternate pulls of the risers. His black boots stood out in stark relief against the snowcaps. The mountains now surrounded him, and he watched as the ground rushed toward him.

Bolan brought the chute into a small field maybe one hundred yards from his opponent's landing site. He hit the ground, performed an expert fall and rolled out of it to land on his feet.

The warrior slapped the quick-disconnects on the chute harness and unslung his Galil. He sprinted out of the clearing, his boots crunching on the inch of snow that covered the clearing, entered the wood line and continued in the direction of his target.

Bolan was within fifty yards of the drop zone when his eye caught the chute. It was below the tree line but had hung on a set of lower branches. An empty harness dangled from the chute about ten feet above the ground.

The enemy was close; the hunt was on.

THE ONLY THING the sleepy little town of Poncha Springs lacked was excitement, and that didn't bother Caleb Durning one bit. He and Debbie had run their little bed-and-breakfast cabin on the outskirts of the city that was located at the crossroads of U.S. Highways 50 and 285.

Poncha Springs was at the center of Fourteener Country. In the 1840s, Kit Carson had explored the area and discovered the hot water springs under the use and protection of the Ute Indians. It was natural Poncha Springs would become a white settler's dream. A good portion of the small town's income was based on industry and the pipeline that ran from those springs to the Salida Hot Springs Aquatic Center.

Many important and historic figures had stayed in the area, such as Susan B. Anthony, Teddy Roosevelt, and even Frank and Jesse James. It was rugged mountain country, practically untouched by the tentacles of modern civilization.

This was a big season for the Durnings. They owned three log cabins that featured plenty of space, a warm bed and three hot meals a day. Debbie loved to cook and Caleb loved to eat, so theirs was a match made in heaven.

Caleb stood from where he'd been stooped over cutting firewood. He laid down his ax and rubbed at the soreness in his lower back. He would turn fifty-six this year—not the strong and wiry man he'd once been—but he enjoyed hard work and believed in living life to the fullest.

Caleb squinted and shaded his eyes against the sun when movement caught his eye. He looked toward the foothills behind the cabin. A solitary figure was quickly making its way down the mountainside and Caleb was puzzled. He wasn't used to seeing that many people out this way. As the figure drew closer, Caleb could discern odd clothing. It looked the person was wearing tan, brown and white camouflage.

There was something in his hand and Caleb strained his eyes further.

It was a gun!

Caleb was immediately suspicious. If there was anything he couldn't stand, it was a poacher. He watched the man approach him. It looked as if he were limping. He wondered if perhaps the man had simply been hiking and injured himself somehow. Well, Caleb Durning would find out just what the heck was going on.

The man reached the bottom of the hill and walked in his direction. As he drew nearer, Caleb reached down to the ax and hefted it confidently in his hands. He quickly fixed the features in his mind. The man was lithe and muscular, a might smaller than he was, with muscular arms and dark hair. His skin was dark, as well. He looked like an Arab, and Caleb's curiosity was aroused.

"Hey there, fella," Caleb said. "What's going on?"

"I do not have time to explain," the man said. "Do you have a vehicle?"

"Maybe," Caleb replied slowly. He gripped the ax tightly. "Where did you come from?"

"Take me to your vehicle please."

"Now just wait a minute there, buddy—"

The man stepped forward and raised his pistol.

Caleb had seen quite a few guns in his time, and he even owned a revolver. Debbie wasn't much for guns, but Caleb kept one around for protection against bears and the like. He wished he had the dratted thing now, although he didn't know if he could have used it on another human being.

"O-okay," Caleb stammered, "what do you want? Take anything you want, okay? Ju-just don't hurt me or my wife."

"Do as you are told, sir," the man replied, "and you will not get hurt. Take me to your vehicle."

Caleb nodded and started to lower the ax and turn as if to cooperate. He continued to drop the ax to the ground until his back was to the man. The rear door of the cabin opened at that moment and his wife stepped onto the porch.

"Caleb Durning?" she demanded. "Now I know you heard me calling you for lunch, and... Oh!"

"Debbie! Call the sheriff!" Caleb screamed.

He hefted the ax and swung it in a circle. The ax head whistled with the blinding speed. For an older man, Caleb Durning could still hold his own with the best of them. There was no way he was about to let this man hurt him or his family. If he died in the attempt, so be it, but he wasn't going to just lie down and show his belly like some scared dog.

As the ax reached the gunman, Caleb saw a flash from the barrel.

20

Ilia Yasso's stomach churned as the C-141 pitched and rolled on a descent course.

A wave of nausea rolled over her, the result of fumes that spilled into the cargo hold. Through a side view port, Yasso could see the damaged engines. The pilots were fighting to bring the plane down, and the Mossad woman was grateful that they hadn't elected to bail out like Mendel.

The Kahane terrorist had gotten away, and that made her angry enough to stifle the fear she felt at the present situation. A howling wind rushed through the gaping hole left by Mendel's departure. She wished the pilots would close the blasted thing, but they were probably more concerned with preserving their lives.

Yasso couldn't escape the morbid thought that she might die this day. Even as she was tossed from side to side, her dark hair whipped by the buffeting winds, her thoughts turned to Pollock. She wondered if he had survived his battle against the remaining Kahane terrorists. He was a survivor, no matter what the odds.

She had fought beside this man. He had protected her, and she felt a renewed strength coming to her mind and body. If the plane crashed and she perished, Yasso wouldn't consider it a loss. Mendel had unwittingly delivered the chips into her hands. She turned to see the innocent-looking crate secured at the front of the cargo hold.

She had accomplished her mission. It would be for the betterment of her country, and she was confident Israel would survive. Her people had survived for many centuries against all odds, and her death wouldn't be untimely. Something good would result from her determination. They would recover the ACTEN technology, and Baram Herzhaft's creation wouldn't fall into the hands of the Kach-Kahane movement.

She could find solace in that thought.

Nonetheless, she wasn't about to resign herself to the ultimate fate yet.

Yasso wondered what Pollock would do.

The answer suddenly appeared when she felt something tap the side of her boot. She looked down and noticed a first-aid kit that had worked its way loose from the opposite wall. Perhaps there was something inside of it she could use to cut through the heavy rope around her wrists.

There was a chance, however slim it might be.

She slid the kit between her feet and used the edge of her boot to pry up a lever at the front. The kit popped open and Yasso saw her saving grace. It was lying there innocently—a surgical scalpel. She slid the box against the wall where she was tied and managed to tip it until the scalpel fell out. She wedged the surgical instrument between her boots.

Muscles strained as Yasso grabbed the handhold to which she was tied and lifted her feet off the ground. She placed the soles of her boots flat against the wall and began to inch her legs up until they reached her hands. She twisted her wrist downward and grabbed the handle of the scalpel.

Yasso tore the paper covering from the device with her teeth and used her thumb to pop the clear plastic sheath from the blade. The sharp razor glinted in the lights. The Mossad agent twisted the scalpel upside down and began to saw through her bonds. Within a minute, her hands were free.

Yasso turned to look out the back of the plane and saw the trees brush past just beneath the cargo door. She quickly ran to it and engaged the lift. The ramp began to rise obediently as she turned and raced to the jump seat. Yasso fastened the lap belt, pulled the shoulder harness down and clipped the ratchet into a slot above the lap buckle.

The wings began to whistle and the nose started to lift as the C-141 crashed through the forest. The port engines powered up as the pilots reversed thrust. Tree branches snapped under the force of the wings and the cargo plane vibrated with the merciless punishment.

Yasso began to pray earnestly.

She opened her eyes and looked out the window next to her. Flames erupted from one of the port engines, and the C-141 began to drop like a stone. It plummeted through the brush and Yasso's eyes widened with surprise as a clearing replaced the forestry.

The plane hit the ground hard, and Yasso clenched her teeth as the impact rode up her tailbone and into her spine. Windows imploded and glass flew into her hair. Several of the jagged shards cut her skin, and blood began to run from the wounds.

The C-141 bounced into the air and came down with comparative force to the first impact. Yasso could feel the rear end begin to yaw and the plane started to slide on its belly. Some unseen force suddenly sent the huge aircraft into the air. Her stomach rolled as the C-141 flipped.

The starboard wing collapsed, and its heavy metal frame punctured the hull.

Metal and debris flew through the plane in crisscross patterns, and smoke began to fill the hold. Yasso choked on the acrid fumes as the plane continued a dizzying roll. She wasn't sure how many times they tumbled, but the plane finally came to a halt in an upright position.

Yasso felt a new pain in her thigh. She looked down in horror to find a large piece of metal had gone through her leg and embedded itself in the seat beneath. There was very little blood, and she hoped the pole had missed vital arteries and veins. It appeared to have lodged in the meaty portion of her thigh, and with a pounding heart Yasso figured there was a chance she might survive.

If she could get out of this predicament.

The smoke began to thicken, and a tremendous buildup of heat touched her skin. Somewhere inside the hold, a fire had broken out. She would die if she didn't do something. She hadn't freed herself from the ropes only to burn to death inside this metal tomb.

The Mossad agent took several deep breaths and began to whimper as she wrapped her hands around the pole. It was going to hurt, but there weren't a whole lot of options. She took one last breath and yanked with all her might. The pole slid from the seat, and Yasso nearly passed out with the waves of agony that racked her leg as she withdrew the smooth metal.

She took another deep breath and tried to will life-giving oxygen to her body. Tears fell from her cheeks as she slid out of her shirt and wrapped the wound, tying a double knot tightly over the gaping hole in her thigh.

Yasso tried to rise, but the leg wouldn't support her. She reached down and grabbed the pole. She leaned on it and rested the majority of her small frame on the good leg. The choking smoke threatened to overtake her, but Yasso pushed herself to escape from the wreckage.

She managed to find the rear of the cargo hold and yanked down on the ramp control. The ramp fell about a quarter of the way before it failed to budge farther.

Yasso smiled. God was favoring her this time.

She crawled up the ramp on her belly and reached the top with a considerable effort. The smoke began to clear, replaced by fresh air and daylight outside. Yasso rolled over the edge of the ramp and fell to the ground outside.

She could hear the sound of rotor blades just before she fell unconscious.

KURTZMAN HAD DONE IT!

Fort Carson was online, and its computers were humming at peak efficiency. Wasserman had downgraded the alert status of the post, and they were awaiting the arrival of federal investigators. There was still a tremendous amount of work to be done, but the immediate disaster had been averted.

Brognola was as proud as a peacock as he shook the computer whiz's hand.

"That was a damned fine job, Aaron," the head Fed boomed.

"Thanks, Hal." A concerned expression replaced Kurtzman's grin. "Has there been any more word?"

"Grimaldi says the plane came down hard, but there's a good portion of it intact. They're working on the wreckage now to see if they can recover the chips and the friendly Striker said might be aboard."

Kurtzman nodded. "I'm just glad to hear he's okay."

"Yes," Brognola said quietly. "So am I."

Wasserman entered his office with Dunham in tow and went to drop into his chair. He stared at the Stony Man crew with admiration. There was a long and respectful silence as the four men considered the events of the past twenty-four hours. There had been plenty of sorrow and bloodshed.

The Kahane Chai was far from defeated, but Brognola felt it was a step in the right direction. They had come face-to-face with a brand-new enemy, and the Stony Man chief was certain that this wouldn't be the last time they encountered the terror group.

Moreover, Brognola could only hope the Executioner would be there to fight them.

"I don't think there are words that can express my gratitude to you and your people, Brognola," Wasserman said humbly.

"The fact we were able to restore your system is enough," Brognola replied. "I appreciate your cooperation, General."

"You know," Wasserman said offhandedly, "I'm sure the place you guys come from isn't even on the books. Nevertheless, if you ever need anything from me, and I mean *anything,* don't hesitate to call. The Army owes you a considerable debt."

Brognola waved it away. "Let's hope we never have to collect on that one."

The four men looked at each other in silence again. It was a moment to reflect on the departed, and to consider the far-reaching consequences of battling the effects of terrorism.

And Brognola couldn't help but spare a thought for the Executioner.

Wherever he was.

MACK BOLAN EMERGED from the wood line as the crack from a gun echoed along the hillside.

The soldier saw a large, burly man stagger and fall, then the Kahane leader hobbled past his victim in the direction of a log cabin.

The Executioner launched himself down the hillside. There was no way the terrorist was going to claim any more victims today. He sprinted at full speed, the wind rushing in his ears as he crossed the expanse. Bolan leaped over large rocks or jumped around scattered brush and trees as he descended.

Less than a minute had elapsed by the time he reached the quivering form that lay on the ground. The victim was an older man, maybe fifty-five, and blood was running freely from his right shoulder. Bolan reached into the first-aid pouch on his combat harness and whipped out a compress.

Grateful eyes stared back at the Executioner as the older man smiled at him.

"I'll be okay, soldier," the man said. "Just don't let him hurt my Debbie. Please—" His pleas were cut short by a groan.

"You can bet on it," Bolan whispered tightly.

The Executioner rose and turned in the direction of the cabin. He could feel the rage swelling inside of him and he forced it back. He marched toward the house in purposeful and powerful strides. Even as he reached the back door, he could hear the struggles inside.

Bolan found the terrorist leader standing over the man's

terrified spouse. She was screaming for help, the receiver of a wall-mounted telephone still clutched in her hand. The Kahane terrorist bent over her and tried to stifle her screams. His hand covered her mouth, and he was attempting to ward her off as she began to beat him with the remnants of the telephone.

"Just give me the keys to your vehicle, bitch!" he screamed.

Suddenly, he reached into the pocket of her housedress and found a set of keys. They jangled in Bolan's ears like a thousand bells.

The Executioner started to cross the gap when the terrorist straightened, whirled and aimed his pistol at him. Bolan dived to the floor as the gunman fired two shots over his head. Chips of plaster and paint rained on the soldier. He rolled behind the cover of the couch before his enemy could draw a new bead on him.

The Kahane terrorist turned and rushed out the front door.

Bolan regained his feet and paused at the door to whisper a brief reassuring word to the woman. Then he continued through the doorway and stepped onto the front porch. The Kahane leader had slid behind the wheel of an old, dilapidated pickup truck.

Bolan tossed his Galil aside and drew the .44 Desert Eagle. He placed two quick shots in the front tires and one in the grille. The terrorist still appeared to be fumbling with the lock inside.

He couldn't seem to find the right key.

The Kahane leader looked up with wide eyes as Bolan stepped off the porch and began to walk toward him. The terrorist raised his pistol and fired three shots, but his nerves were now shattered, and he couldn't seem to hit the specter that loomed ever closer.

Bolan heard the rounds whiz past his ears.

The Jericho 941 pistol locked back on an empty chamber.

The terrorist climbed out on the passenger side and ducked behind the vehicle to reload. The Executioner launched himself across the arid ground and leaped into the back of the pickup. He crossed the bed and dropped to the ground on the other side.

The Kahane leader stared up at Bolan as he slammed the magazine into the handgrip.

The gaping muzzle of the Desert Eagle stared back at him.

"You're not that fast," the Executioner said quietly.

"You are correct, Pollock," the man replied in an even tone.

"And who the hell are you?"

He shrugged. "It is not important."

"Was it worth it?" Bolan asked. "Was it worth all the people who have died over this?"

"The Kach-Kahane Chai brotherhood will go on. For every one of us you destroy, two will replace him. It is unavoidable. We will succeed against you, and your nation will fall with the pathetic patriots of Islam."

"What about Yasso? Is she dead?"

The man threw his head back and laughed. "Of course."

"I see."

"No, you do not see, Pollock. You are as blind as the rest of your countrymen. You would attempt to defy what God has already ordained. It is He who gives us power and it is He who predetermines our paths. I am honored to die for His cause. For you and your government, it will not end with my death. It will just begin. There is no hope."

"Not for you," Bolan growled.

The Executioner squeezed the trigger. The man's head exploded from the impact, crushing his skull and blowing his brains across the gravel drive. Some of the spatter landed on the side of the truck. A grim reminder that injustice against the helpless and murder of the innocent would not go unpunished by the Executioner.

He holstered his weapon and took a deep breath.

Bolan searched the body for identification, but there was none. Stony Man would eventually discover his identity, although they would probably have to do it through fingerprints or dental records. There was very little left of the Kahane leader's head.

The dead man now lying before him had been right, and Mack Bolan knew it. It wasn't going to end with the death of one or two. As he considered the past day or two, he realized a new challenge had come to rear its gruesome head.

Terrorism was terrorism, whether by another name or another method. It didn't change with groups or ideologies—it didn't change with technologies. There was a reason he'd labeled his war as everlasting, and the Kach-Kahane Chai movement was just one more hand dealt into the game. They were one more head that he would chop off at the neck, and hope something new didn't emerge in its place.

But until the day the bullet found its mark, Mack Bolan would be there to face every new challenge. He would come in fighting and he would ram his own ideas right down their throats. He would give them no quarter, no rest. They would never be safe from him. There was no place they could hide—not even behind a computer.

He would rain the ultimate destruction right down on top of their heads, and he wouldn't stop until the evil and hatred burned in the ashes. Justice by fire until every terrorist and criminal was eradicated from the face of his planet—every drug pusher, terror monger, murderer and victimizer of a free society. He would fight until they vowed never to return.

But for the moment, it was over.

The Executioner turned and walked away.

TAKE 'EM FREE
2 action-packed novels plus a mystery bonus
NO RISK
NO OBLIGATION TO BUY